MURDER
SO FIENDISH

MURDER SO FIENDISH

A Merry March Mystery

Eileen Curley Hammond

Twody Press

Cover designed by SelfPubBookCovers.com/ RLSather

Eileen Curley Hammond
Visit my website at www.eileencurleyhammond.com

Printed in the United States of America

First Printing: November 2022
Twody Press, West Jefferson OH

ISBN-978-1-956356-02-1
Library of Congress Control Number: 2022920056

AUTHOR'S NOTE

Thank you, readers, for spending your time with Merry—if you like her stories, I'd appreciate it if you'd take a moment to write a review on Amazon or Goodreads.

An author's journey is somewhat solitary, but I've been lucky to have friends who help along the way. Specifically, I'd like to thank Jenna Grinstead, who has a keen eye for repetitive words and for when I forget to wring enough emotion out of a scene. I'd also like to thank Eric Henderson for his strong sense of flow and ability to catch typos. In addition, I genuinely appreciate the Buckeye Crime Writers group (especially the Board) for their advice and motivation.

I also thank my terrific editor, Bambi Sommers, for her guidance, polishing ability, and patience with the typical back-and-forth of book publishing.

In addition, much appreciation to my brother-in-law, Jim Silvey, for giving me an exciting challenge to weave into this book and my sister Caroline Silvey for sharing her cruise ship experiences.

Any errors in the book are mine and mine alone.

And finally, thank you to the rest of my family and husband for their unwavering support.

ALSO BY EILEEN CURLEY HAMMOND

Murder So Sinful
Murder So Festive
Murder So Heartless
Murder So Deadly
Murder So Hot
Murder So Tempting

For writers and friends who left us far too soon this year:
Dawn Hosmer, Carolyn Melvin, and Uncle Jim.

Chapter 1

Jenny lifted my chin. "Are you nervous?" Her long blond hair was captured in a graceful chignon, and her face shimmered from the barest hint of glitter the make-up artist had incorporated.

I held back tears, studying my tall, graceful seventeen-year-old daughter, who looked far older today. "I'm fine. I love Rob and can't wait to be married to him."

The make-up artist cleared her throat. "Just a few minutes longer. No crying, or you'll ruin all my work."

"No promises." I stifled a laugh.

My best friend, Patty, walked into the room. Her long brown hair spilled over the shoulder of her sleeveless turquoise gown. "Church is filling up. It's almost show time."

"I still need to get formal shots," the photographer huffed.

"Almost done." The make-up artist swiped blush on my cheeks and gave my lips one more pass. She lifted the sheet, which had been covering my dress, and I stood.

"Wowza." Patty smiled. "That dress really works with your red hair and creamy complexion."

I rushed to the mirror. "I hope I don't look too fake." My mouth dropped. I was me, but so much better. She had emphasized my large green eyes with a lavender liner. I turned to the make-up artist. "You are a wizard."

She packed her things. "Don't forget to leave a review."

Jenny stood next to me. "Perfection, Mom. That dress was made for you."

My gown had a fitted bodice of muted pastels, teal, and rose, encapsulated by fine silver thread. The floor-length bottom was cream-colored chiffon. Patty and Jenny were equally stunning in their simple, matching turquoise ones. Jenny's was set apart with the special sash the clothing store had made using all of the colors of my dress.

The photographer tapped his watch. "Need to get a move on."

We posed for what seemed like a million pictures, and then there was a rap on the door. The parish assistant, Belinda, stuck her head in. "It's time."

I squeezed Jenny's hand. "You ready?"

She nodded.

Patty hugged me and slid my round bouquet of deep orange and red roses interspersed with dark evergreen foliage into my hand. It was perfect for a wedding the weekend before Thanksgiving.

She said, "Let's go."

Patty walked out first, then Jenny and I followed, regrouping just out of sight under the stairs leading to the choir loft above the narthex. Pachelbel's Canon began, and Patty started her stutter step down the aisle. I placed my hand inside Jenny's arm, and we began our slow procession.

I was thrilled someone's schedule changed so we could get married in the afternoon on Saturday instead of Friday night—the church was lovely in the daytime. Stained-glass windows diffused the sunlight, giving the church a rosy hue and making the white runner shine, while simple burgundy bows adorned with fall leaves decorated the polished oak pews.

Rob stood tall but was a little pale, blond hair neatly shorn, waiting at the front. His face lit with a broad grin when he saw me, making his mustache twitch. I started to tear, and Jenny whispered, "Make-up."

I chuckled, which helped.

Friends nodded and smiled as we made our way to the front, and my neighbors, Ed and Andy, blew me a kiss. Finally, I stood in front of Rob, with Jenny in between us.

The music stopped, and Jenny said, "Robert Jenson, I invite you to join our family, to be part of our ups and downs, and to love us with all your heart."

His voice cracked as he said, "I accept your invitation."

Rob and I hugged her, and she stepped back and sat with Rob's mother, her husband, and their niece, Amy, who had opted not to be in the wedding after everything that had happened earlier in the fall.

I clasped Rob's hand and grinned at his best person, his sister, Elizabeth, regal in her dark eggplant-colored chiffon, and he and I turned to Father Tom, who beamed as he began the ceremony. Overcome with emotion and thinking of all we had been through in the past year, it went quickly. I was wrenched back to the present when Father Tom intoned, "If anyone objects to the marriage, speak now or forever hold your peace."

A door slammed, and Father Tom paled. Patty turned and gasped, so Rob and I pivoted. My ex, Drew, was at the back of the church with his girlfriend, Arianna. He gave a half-hearted wave with his trademark lazy smile and said, "No objections here," as they slid into the back pew.

The congregation began to murmur as we turned around to face the priest, and Rob mouthed, "What the heck?"

I squeezed my eyes shut and muttered, "Could this get any more cliché?" My face grew hot as my blood pressure rose. *How had they gotten out of prison? What was going on? And why were they here, of all places?*

Father Tom cleared his throat and resumed the ceremony as my stomach churned. I glanced at Jenny, who couldn't stop turning around to stare at her father. Patty grabbed my other hand and whispered, "Focus."

We said our vows, then Elizabeth gave Rob my ring, and he placed it on my hand, saying, "With this ring comes my love."

Patty handed me Rob's ring, and my fingers shook as I slid it onto his finger. "With this ring, you join our family."

Father Tom said, "I now pronounce you husband and wife. You may kiss the bride."

Rob kissed me, and the congregation clapped. The Brandenburg Concerto played, and Rob and I walked down the aisle, stopping to invite Jenny to join us and to give Rob's mother and stepfather a kiss.

Rob glared at Drew as we passed their aisle, and then we formed a receiving line in the narthex. Jenny hugged Rob and me as she exclaimed, "How is Dad here? Did you know he was coming?"

My lips thinned as I shook my head. "I was just as surprised as you."

Rob's mother and stepfather hugged us and joined the receiving line. His mother, Wanda, who wore a lavender, slim-fitting couture suit, said, "Lovely ceremony, but who were the couple who came in so late?"

"My ex and his girlfriend." I gritted my teeth.

"Not very good taste inviting your ex, even if you've both moved on." She turned to greet one of her and Mac's friends.

I was happy to see Wanda had recovered from her stroke with minimal impact, but she still had a way of getting under my skin. *Like I would've invited Drew.*

Our neighbors, Ed and Andy, offered hugs and congratulations. Andy whispered in my ear, "Such a surprise to see Drew here. And with his usual impeccable timing." He chuckled as he left the church.

The rest of the crowd funneled past and offered congratulations on their way to the reception. Finally, Drew and Arianna arrived. Drew was his usual suave self, but Arianna was gaunt, her normally lustrous black locks lank against her too-large navy suit.

Jenny eyed me, almost like she was waiting for permission. I shrugged, and she ran into Drew's arms. "I'm so glad to see you!"

"What are you doing here, Drew?" Rob asked, his voice sharper than a razor.

"Not happy to see me?" Drew laughed.

We stared at him.

"DA planted evidence in a case, and now everything he was working on is under scrutiny. Luckily, my very well-paid lawyer made the case that we shouldn't have to cool our heels in jail till they straighten everything out." He shrugged.

My mouth dropped. "But aren't they worried you'll take off?"

"Can't go far." He lifted his pant leg to display a tracking monitor.

"But why here?" Rob objected.

Drew pointed to Jenny. "If we have to stay in the United States, I want to be near my daughter." He cleared his throat. "And I have a favor to ask. They froze our assets, but I still have a few irons in the fire. That means it's going to take me a few weeks to get access to funds. So, I thought since you're going on your honeymoon, our house would be empty. Problem solved."

I took a calming breath and counted to five. "First, it's my house, not our house. And second, no."

"Please? That way, I could see him and Arianna all the time." Jenny pleaded.

The photographer touched Rob's elbow. "Sorry to interrupt, but we only have a little bit of time before the reception. We need to get started."

Rob said, "Drew, you and Arianna can stay at my place. I've already moved a lot of my stuff to Merry's over the past day or two." He handed them the keys and gave them the address.

Jenny threw her arms around Rob. "Thanks, Rad. You're the best."

"Rad?" Drew's eyebrow rose.

"Mix of Rob and Dad." Jenny kissed Drew's cheek. "You and Arianna need to leave now. I'll see you tomorrow."

"Are you sure you don't want me to stay for pictures?" Drew chuckled as Rob grew red.

Arianna yanked on Drew's arm. "Leaving now. Thanks for the place to stay."

Chapter 2

Our taxi drew close to the Miami harbor, and one of the ships dwarfed everything near it. I shaded my eyes. "Which one? That one is huge—must be fourteen stories and quite a few football fields long. It could hold a small city."

Rob pointed. "The one next to her. Serendipity of the Seas."

The ship was far smaller and would fit into the other one twice over with room to spare. The teak banisters gleamed in the sun, and every speck of the white ship shone as if freshly washed. The cab parked, Rob paid, and we got out. Men scurried to the taxi and removed our luggage.

I tucked my hand in his as we walked toward the small line waiting to register before boarding. "I almost hate to say this, but it looks expensive—are you sure we should be spending this kind of money with Jenny going to college next year?"

"First, it's too late now, and second, Mother and Mac insisted that this be their wedding gift."

"Wow. That's really extravagant."

"It is, but they can afford it. And they wanted to do something nice for you after everything that happened. Mother is sure she would have been far worse off had you not been there to protect her."

We moved forward in line, and I said, "She looked like her normal elegant self at the wedding—that place Mac took her to knew what they were doing."

Rob moved toward the now-empty window and handed the waiting woman our passports and paperwork.

"I can't believe you kept this a secret. And I'm glad you told me to wear my dressier shorts and sandals."

"I loved keeping you guessing, and Jenny did too. It was her idea to get the African safari brochure and 'accidentally' leave it in the car. I wouldn't have been able to do any of this without her since she packed for you."

I smiled. "I hope she remembered everything."

"If she's forgotten anything important, we can get it at one of the stops or the ship's gift shop." Rob put his arm around me and pulled me toward him.

"Who am I kidding? She's a better packer than me and has a much more developed sense of style." I chuckled. "At least I can be sure everything matches."

The woman said, "Here are your key cards, shore excursion tickets, and a list of the specialty restaurant reservations you made. Enjoy your cruise."

We followed the signs, riding the escalator and then taking a right to the ship's ramp. As we entered, a man and woman in crisp white dress uniforms greeted us with glasses of champagne. One said, "Cabins will be ready around three—announcements will be made, so please feel free to explore in the meantime. The restaurants on deck eleven are open now."

An enormous crystal chandelier hung over wood-look tile stairs that led to the floor below, the banisters shone like brushed gold, and plush carpets in calming shades of brown abutted the glistening marble floors of the entryway and the reception area. My mouth dropped. "This is beautiful."

Rob kissed the top of my head. "Glad you like it. Want to get something to eat?"

"Starving. They certainly don't feed you on the plane." We entered the glass-enclosed elevator, and I pushed the button for eleven.

When it stopped, we exited and opened the doors to the pool. People rested in their street clothes on vast rows of pillow-topped loungers. Rob said, "One of those may be in my future. We were up pretty late at the reception, and my feet are still sore from dancing."

"I hope you're not implying I stepped on your toes—at least not more than once." I kissed the hand on my shoulder. "It was fun, wasn't it?"

He nodded as we found an open table near the outdoor grill and sat. I perused the menu. "Burgers, chicken, fries, and salads. Oh—they have an ahi tuna burger. That would be better for me." I closed the menu. "Nope. Wedding's over. I'm going with bacon cheeseburger, fries, and a chocolate malt."

"Two." A waiter arrived, and Rob gave him our order.

"I haven't had a chance to thank you for offering your house to Drew and Arianna. That was above and beyond, but you made Jenny happy." I put my hand over his.

"I wasn't going to let him stay in our house. Plus, I wanted to get rid of him. I can't believe he showed up at the wedding—he has a lot of nerve."

"That he does." The malts arrived, and I took a sip. "Yum—packed with ice cream—just the way I like it."

Rob squeezed my hand. "Last time we talk about Drew on this trip."

"Deal—with a caveat—if Jenny has problems with him while we're away, we'll discuss him."

"As a new parent, I agree." He lifted my hand and kissed it.

There was a group of six people a few tables away, and two of them raised their voices. Then a fortyish man whose appearance telegraphed that he'd never seen the inside of a gym stood and threw a punch at the older, seated man. Waiters rushed toward them and escorted the two from the deck. A curvaceous woman in her late thirties with long brown hair, polka-dot sleeveless blouse, stylish shorts, and a Gucci purse realized they were the center of attention and waved her hand dismissively. "Nothing to see here. Just a few dudes who've had too much to drink." She plucked the olive from the skewer in her martini glass, popped it into her mouth, and smiled.

"I didn't know there would be a show at lunch." Rob chuckled.

Our meals arrived, and we ate. Just as we finished, the loudspeaker activated with a chime. "Guests in suites on deck nine may access them now."

Rob kissed my hand. "That's us unless you want something more?"

"I can't wait to see our suite."

He stood and pulled me to my feet. "An invitation if I ever heard one."

We took the wide, lushly carpeted stairs down two flights, found our room, and used the key card to open the door. I said, "Wow. A lot bigger room than Jenny and I had when we went to Alaska."

Rob gave me a gentle kiss. "Happy honeymoon."

There was a rap on the door we had somehow ended up leaning against as our kisses deepened. The steward entered and said, "Welcome, Mr. Jenson and Ms. March. I wanted to introduce myself and tell you a little about the room. The TV comes out and swivels so you can watch it from the bed." He walked toward it and demonstrated. "Balcony is here. Please don't forget to shut the door when you leave the room. And bathroom and closet are here. A complimentary bottle of champagne is chilling on the table, and I've stocked your refrigerator with sodas and beer." He opened the mini refrigerator and paused for a breath. "Is there anything else you would like?"

"You've thought of everything." I smiled.

"More pillows?"

"We're good." Rob walked with him to the door.

"There's a mandatory lifeboat drill at five." The steward pointed to the closet. "Life vests are in there. Please wear them to the drill." He paused. "Would you like me to show you how to put them on?"

Rob opened the door. "We'll figure it out."

"If there's anything, my name is Silvio…"

"Thanks, Silvio." Rob grabbed the do not disturb sign, hung it on the outside knob, and shut the door.

"That was kind of abrupt," I said.

"C'mere, you." Rob pulled me into his arms.

* * *

We arrived at the main restaurant at six-thirty, and there was a line to get in. It was a large space with a cozy appearance because it had been broken into smaller enclaves, denoted by deep off-white scalloped coffered ceilings. Understated round chandeliers hung within each quadrant, lending a shimmering light, and marine blue velvet chairs were pushed with precision against ivory cloths. The tables were set with various wine glasses, water goblets, decorative chargers, and silver cutlery. My stomach growled—if the dining room looked that good, the food must be wonderful.

When we finally approached the desk and gave the woman our suite number, she said, "The first night is always a bit crowded. We don't have a table for two right now and probably won't have one available till around eight. There are several bars on this floor where you can wait."

I turned toward Rob. "You okay with waiting?"

She interjected, "Or, I have a table for eight in our specialty steak restaurant you could join. You'd be with six other people."

"Right now?" Rob asked.

She nodded.

He glanced at me, and I said, "We'll take it."

We went up a floor to Prime and Beyond, and the Maître D' escorted us to the table. The room was like an old-fashioned steak house but lighter, with sumptuous cream leather chairs and generous tables with crisp white linens. Forks, knives, and spoons were lined up, waiting for the eating to begin.

I gripped Rob's hand tighter—the Maître D' was leading us to the group we'd seen arguing earlier in the day, but they seemed in better moods and had cleaned up well. The men wore bespoke muted navy sports jackets, one with dove-gray slacks, the other with brown pants. Both had stomachs that overlapped their belts. We introduced ourselves and sat.

The younger one was around our age, and the other was near seventy, with a spray-on tan and bad comb-over. The older man stuck out his hand. "Butch Calhoun and this is my family. Randy, over there's my son, Sheila's his wife, Becky's my daughter, and that's her quote, friend, unquote, Samantha."

Samantha gave Butch a filthy look and turned to me. "Sam, please, and it's 'partner,' not 'friend.'" She had closely cropped black hair and wore tailored gray slacks, a high-buttoned long-sleeve shirt, and a deep purple jacket.

The father and son were the ones who had been arguing early in the day, and Randy's attractive wife, Sheila, who was poured into her dark green sequined dress, was the woman who had been drinking a martini.

The slender blonde-haired woman next to me seemed five years younger than my thirty-nine and was dressed in a conservative sweater and slacks. I offered my hand. "I don't think you were introduced, I'm Merry March, and this is my husband, Rob. Are you Butch's daughter?"

She shook her head, and her voice quavered. "Dawn. His wife." She sprang from the table, muttering, "Excuse me," as she headed for the exit.

My eyes widened as I started to get up. "Someone should go after her."

Butch laughed. "No need. She'll get over it. She always does."

"I better go." Randy stood and raced from the room.

"Perfect." Sheila twirled the blue cheese stuffed olive in her martini. "Great trip, Butch. Your wife and my husband." She pointed to her drink and beckoned the waiter. "One more."

He nodded. "Will the two be coming back? Would you like to wait?"

"I'm starving. Let's order." Butch gave detailed instructions as to what he wanted and how he wanted it prepared, and then everyone else followed suit.

I regretted our choice to join the table but figured there was no way we could leave now. I pointed to the porterhouse for two and asked Rob, "Want to do that?"

He nodded, and I ordered. After the waiter had taken the menus, I asked, "What does everyone do?"

"Money," Butch said.

I raised my eyebrow.

"Trader. On Wall Street." He sipped bourbon.

"I paint. Oils mostly, love plein air." Becky leaned forward for a dinner roll and deposited it on a plate. She looked like a free spirit, long flowing paisley-print sun dress, minimal makeup, and curly brown hair.

Sam passed her the butter. "I own a gallery—that's how we met." She smiled at Becky.

"I sell insurance," I interjected. "And Rob owns a newspaper."

Sheila glanced at her French-tipped nails. "I like to shop. My husband's a trader like Butch."

"Not one of those obnoxious reporters, are you?" Butch asked Rob. "Always up in somebody's business. Never good news when a reporter calls you."

I felt my face grow hot and leaned forward to defend Rob. He laid his hand on mine and said, "I used to be a global reporter, but now I focus on what's going on in our small town and the surrounding area. I like to think I perform a service."

Butch sniffed and turned his attention to me. "And now I suppose you're going to try and sell me insurance."

13

"I'm not licensed in New York. So, unless you have property in Ohio…" I broke off a piece of a roll and stuck it in my mouth, afraid I'd say something else.

Randy slid back onto his seat, frowning. "Everyone order already?"

"Is little Miss Goody Two-shoes okay?" Sheila sneered.

"Fine. Dad, you really should be nicer to her." The waiter stopped and took Randy's order.

"She coming back?" Butch asked.

Randy shook his head. "She said she'd see everyone tomorrow."

"I guess I'll get a cold shoulder tonight. Good thing there's another bedroom, or it'd be the couch for me." Butch shrugged. "Three days at sea. I'm going to try that new virtual reality game you played today."

"It was fun." Randy nodded.

"Where did you find that?" Rob asked.

"In a room near the gym. You have to sign up, but you can do that online. What's your room number?" Butch lifted his phone.

"Nine twenty-three."

Butch tapped. "I signed you up for the ten o'clock session right after mine."

"Thanks, but—" I wasn't sure that was the way I wanted to spend my morning.

"You need to get into this century." Butch grabbed another roll and buttered it. "You'll love it."

The waiters began to deliver plates to the table, and the conversation moved on.

* * *

"I could get used to this." I popped a piece of buttery danish into my mouth. "Breakfast in the room, coffee, and a handsome man."

"The waiter?"

"You, silly." I leaned across the table, kissed Rob, and then extended my arm. "I can't believe how big this room is. Dresser, big bed that is the most comfortable one I've ever slept in, end tables, a couch, minifridge, and bar, and that's not even including the balcony. And the closet—it's almost as big as the one at home."

"The bathroom is what got me—separate soaking tub and shower. Way more luxury than what I'm used to. When I was in the mountains of Afghanistan, I was lucky if I had my own toilet, let alone running water." Rob finished his coffee.

I popped the last of my danish into my mouth. "When Jenny and I went to Alaska two years ago, our room was half this size, and we didn't have a balcony. We'll have to do something special for Wanda and Mac when we get home."

Rob checked his watch. "We need to get dressed soon."

"Do we have to go?"

"It might be fun." He stood. "And Jenny will be jealous."

I groaned. "She's going to want one. And Christmas is right around the corner."

"Maybe I'll get it for her."

"Too expensive. I don't want you to feel you have to spend a lot of money on her."

"I'm her 'Rad.' I get to spoil her now." Rob smiled as he stood and extended his hand.

I grabbed it and came to my feet. "Quick shower, and I'll be ready."

Thirty minutes later, we arrived at the room Butch described the night before. A sheet of paper on the door listed times and names. Rob went closer. "We're up in five minutes." Two leather armchairs faced a sea-sprayed window a few steps from the room. "Want to sit here?"

I nodded, then walked to a coffee station nearby. "More coffee? It makes lattes."

"With chocolate syrup."

I put a cup under the machine, pressed the buttons and, when full, handed it to Rob. "Your drink, sir."

He laughed and took a sip. "Hits the spot."

There was a high-pitched scream, and I jumped. "What was that?"

The door to the room with the virtual reality equipment was pushed open and hit the wall. Dawn came out, flinging her headset to the ground, "Butch...there's something wrong." She pointed behind her.

Rob leaped up and raced into the room. I grabbed the phone from inside the door, pressed the button for the front desk, and explained what had happened. The desk clerk said they would send the ship's doctor.

Butch's headset was still in place, but he lay splayed on the floor like a toy flung by a child in a fit of pique. Rob knelt and felt for a pulse. Then, a trainer from the gym next door ran in with a defibrillator as Rob began CPR. The trainer took Butch's headset off, ripped Butch's t-shirt to apply the pads, and told Rob to stand back. A shock was delivered. Nothing. Rob began CPR again and, after a moment or two, the trainer again shouted, "Stand back."

This continued until the doctor arrived, knelt by Butch, and listened to his chest with a stethoscope. He shook his head. "He's gone." Butch's eyes were wide open and unseeing. I looked away.

The doctor lifted his walkie-talkie from his belt and spoke quietly, "Operation Rising Star, virtual reality room."

Dawn's arms were clasped around her body. I touched her elbow and led her to the seats we had been in previously, out of sight of Butch, and asked, "What happened?"

She shook her head. "I don't know. Butch wanted to play the same game, but his didn't sound interesting. I was exploring a desk, searching for clues, and there was a weird kind of squeak and then a thud. I asked Butch if he was okay, but he didn't answer, so I took my headset off, and..." Her voice quavered, and her eyes grew large. "He was just lying there..."

I patted her hand. "You've had a big shock. Can I call someone for you? Would you like coffee or tea?"

"How am I going to tell them? It's all my fault."

Chapter 3

I fiddled with the coffee machine and poured in two sugar packets, figuring Dawn needed it. "What do you mean? How could this be your fault?"

"He has high blood pressure, and we had another fight this morning." She wiped her eyes. "Call Randy—he'll help me. He's in suite nine-fifty."

"Drink this." I handed her the coffee, walked to the phone, and dialed. "Randy, this is Merry March. We met last night."

"Yes?"

"There's been an incident in the virtual reality room. Dawn is asking for you."

"I'll be right there."

A woman who said she was a cruise line customer care representative arrived and sat with Dawn, then a man in white dress with impressive epaulets came up the stairs. I pointed toward the room. "My husband, Rob, is with him."

He walked past, and I followed, closing the door after me. The doctor and Rob were talking quietly—the trainer had left the room when the doctor got there to go back to the gym. Rob held out his hand to the new arrival. "Rob Jenson, and that's my wife, Merry March." He pointed to me.

"Chief Security Officer Patterson."

Randy burst into the room. "Dad!" He fell to his knees and tried to embrace Butch.

The doctor said, "Don't touch him."

"Why not? What happened?" Randy got to his feet.

"Not sure. I'll need to examine the body. Who are you?"

"Randy Calhoun, this is my father. What could have caused this?"

The doctor shook his head. "Likely cardiac, but don't know for sure. Don't worry. I'll examine your father fully once I get him downstairs." He paused for a beat and said, "I'm sorry for your loss."

Two crewmen moved Butch onto a stretcher, covered him with a sheet, and took him from the room. Randy walked out behind them, and then the doctor and the officer left the room, conferring quietly. Rob picked up the headset the trainer had taken from Butch and put it on.

"What are you doing?" I whispered.

He paled, jumped back, and tore the headset off.

Chief Security Officer Patterson came back and held out his hand. "I'll take that. This area will be off-limits for at least the rest of the day while we investigate, so I'm going to have to ask you to leave."

Rob handed him the headset. "You may want to see what he saw."

The officer walked to the table with sanitizing wipes and used one. Then, he donned the apparatus. "What am I supposed to see?"

"A huge snake." Rob moved closer to him.

I gasped.

"Nothing on here except for the main menu." The officer took off the headset and shrugged. "Not sure what you think you saw, but it's not there now."

"I didn't think I saw it—I did see it." Rob took the headset from the officer and put it back on. Then he took it off. "You're right—it's the menu. How could it just disappear?"

The officer shrugged.

"Let's go, Merry." Rob laced his fingers with mine.

19

I stopped by the chairs Dawn and Randy were sitting in. "We're so sorry for your loss, and please let us know if there's anything we can do."

Dawn stared at me, but it didn't seem like her eyes were focused. Randy said, "Thanks," and returned his attention to the customer care representative.

Rob pulled on my hand, so I followed him to the elevator and asked, "Why on earth did you put the headset on?"

"Curious."

"You saw a snake?" I shuddered.

"Giant. Bright green—iridescent—and matte black button eyes, with fangs this big." Rob moved his hands to measure about five inches. "And it was about to strike me."

Chapter 4

We returned to our room, and I picked up the information packet on the desk. Flipping through, I found the brochure that touted the virtual reality games as Rob peered over my shoulder. I handed it to him. "I don't know a lot about this, but I don't see one advertising a snake."

"It was there. I don't know why it was gone when the chief security officer checked, but I saw it." He scanned the document. "Who knows? It might be something within one of these. All I can tell you was it shocked the heck out of me. It was so real. Those eyes. And the fangs. I was sure it was going to bite me."

"It's strange they'd have something like that on a ship. I'd think they'd have a written warning. What if a kid saw that—they'd be up for weeks."

"I wish I hadn't seen it." He shook his head.

I plopped onto the sofa. "What are they going to do with his body? You don't think they'd store it with the food?" My eyes widened.

"No way. Too many rules and regulations. This is like a small floating city. They have medical staff on board—maybe they have a morgue."

I shuddered. "Not something I want to imagine."

"Let's not focus on that. We have a day at sea. What would you like to do?" He sat next to me.

I pulled out my phone and tapped into it.

Rob's eyebrow rose to a sharp point.

"Reserved the virtual reality room for tomorrow. I want to see if we can find that game. As for today, I made an appointment for a couple's massage this afternoon. We'll need it after this morning."

"When did you do that?"

"While you were showering this morning. I thought it would be a treat."

"It will be. Let's get our suits on and see if there are empty chaises on the pool deck." He stood and walked to the bag with sunscreen. "Going to need this."

We changed and made our way to the top deck. Two chairs abutted each other with side tables next to them in a sea of people working on their tans. I claimed one of the chaises, and Rob sat next to me. The shapely woman on the next lounger had a large straw hat covering her face and, judging from the pineapple and maraschino cherry skewer jutting from the hurricane glass with white contents, had a pina colada on the table in between us. I placed the sunscreen and my book on my half of the table and then turned toward Rob. "It's crowded, but the sun feels like heaven."

"Anywhere with you is pure bliss." Rob rolled onto his side, facing me, and kissed my hand.

I smiled. "I'm glad you're still happy you married me, even though we're only on day three."

"Best days of my life."

I frowned.

He touched my shoulder. "Not for you?"

"Of course, I'm happy. Delirious even."

His face relaxed into a broad smile.

"I'm just worried about leaving Jenny for Thanksgiving. It's our first holiday apart. I hope she's okay."

"She'll be fine. She's going to be with Patty and her family. And Drew and Arianna are there."

I rubbed Rob's leg with my foot. "I thought we weren't going to talk about Drew."

"We're not. We're going to talk about us." He kissed my nose.

"Doesn't sound that interesting."

"We don't always have to talk." He wiggled his eyebrows. "But for now, my book is calling. The hero is just about to break up an international smuggling ring."

I lifted my mystery and opened it. The main character was racing down a deserted, dark path by a canal when—

"Merry, is that you?" Sheila Calhoun sat up and removed her large hat. She waved toward a waiter and pointed at her now empty glass.

He nodded at her and asked me. "May I get you anything?"

"Club soda, lime, please. Rob, would you like anything?"

"A beer and ice water, thanks."

The waiter walked away, and I turned to Sheila. "I'm sorry about your father-in-law."

"Bad ticker. Figured it was going to happen someday." She shrugged and then tapped my book with her fingernail. "Any good?"

I nodded. "I'm surprised you're here. Your husband seemed so shaken."

"I'm sure he and the merry widow are busy consoling themselves. Besides which, they were talking with the attorney. He's a hottie, but all that stuff is boring. Just tell me what we get and when we're getting it."

My mouth dropped. How could this woman be so insensitive? I opened my book and lifted it, hoping she'd take the hint.

"Butch always insisted an attorney travel with him. And then he'd complain about it. Freeloaders, he'd say. I almost felt sorry for them. Having to be at his beck and call twenty-four, seven. But I guess they chose that life when they took him on as a client."

The waiter arrived with our drinks and handed them to us. I squeezed the lime and took a sip of club soda. "I'm sorry. I missed that. His attorney is here? On the boat?"

"Didn't I just say that?" She batted her eyes at Rob.

He returned his attention to his book.

"He wasn't at dinner with you last night."

"Why would he have been? Honey, he may be dreamy, but he's still hired help." She glanced at her watch. "I suppose I should go down. Don't want that husband of mine to think he can do without me." She stood, donned a black lace cover-up, and left.

"Not the most pleasant person," Rob quipped.

"Got that right. Can you imagine traveling with your lawyer?"

"I'd much rather travel with you." He clinked his glass with mine.

We had a light lunch delivered to our chairs so we wouldn't have to move. I picked at a shrimp and crab salad, while Rob opted for a hot dog and fries. After he finished, he groaned, "I swear I'll start eating healthy again soon."

My book called, and I soon lost myself in the mystery, tuning out the noise of people splashing in the pool until the alarm rang, waking Rob, who had opted to snooze after lunch.

"Spa time." I slipped my feet into flip-flops, donned my cover up, and deposited my book into the bag Rob had extended.

"Ready?" He asked.

"This is the life."

We took the elevator to five and wandered to the other end of the boat. It was apparently the grand opening of the spa because they had a dolphin ice sculpture and a tuxedoed man handing out glasses of champagne. Rob and I both took one, and he lifted his glass, "To us."

"Ms. March?" A petite Asian woman stood in front of us.

I nodded.

"My name is Aishwarya. I will be performing your massage today. This way to the ladies changing room. Mr. Jenson, the men's changing room is right there."

I followed her as she pointed out the various amenities—sauna, steam room, and the area with showers and toilets. She led me to a locker and said, "When you are ready, meet me through these doors."

I removed my clothes, donned the robe hanging in the locker, and then exited the ladies' lounge to the back of the ship. It had a small plunge pool you climbed to enter and various lounges for couples and singles. I stood by the railing, watching the navy rolling waves and making darn sure my robe held closed in the wind.

"Pretty, isn't it?" Rob put his arms around me.

"Ms. March, Mr. Jenson? Ready for you now."

We followed the therapist into the room, which was scented with lavender. Soft oriental tones emerged from the speakers, and the masseuse said, "I'll give you a moment to get under the covers, face down, please." She left the room, and we hung our robes on the hooks provided, put our spa slippers under the tables, and slid under the covers. After a moment, she knocked, and I called, "We're ready."

She came in with another therapist and introduced her. "This is Priyanka, and she will be giving Mr. Jenson's massage."

Aishwarya inserted a small pillow under my ankles and began rubbing the back of my left leg. For a small person, she had very firm hands. I said, "A little softer, please—I'm kind of a wimp."

Rob quipped to his therapist, "I'm not—you can go to town on me."

The sweet almond smell of the oil mingled with the lavender scent of the room, combined with soothing soft music and the massage, made me so relaxed I fell asleep, only waking when the therapist asked us to turn over. As she worked on my shoulders, any tension left from the wedding melted away. All too soon, it was over, and the therapists left the room. I sat up slowly and reached for my robe. "That was the best."

"Um-hum," Rob murmured as he slid on sandals. "Could you learn to do that?"

I laughed. "As soon as you do."

Aishwarya knocked, entered the room, and handed us glasses of ice-cold water with cucumber slices floating in them. "Be sure to drink plenty of water today. I'll show you back to the locker rooms."

* * *

Pale sun peaked through the blackout curtains in the room, and I tiptoed to the drapes, parting them just enough to spy through. Dolphins raced the ship, dodging and weaving, and I could just make out land in the distance. Rob came up behind me and enveloped me with his arms. "What are you doing?"

"Watching dolphins."

He pulled the curtains wider. "Where?"

I pointed.

We stood mesmerized for a while, and then Rob asked, "What time does breakfast arrive?"

I glanced at the clock. "Not for another forty-five minutes."

"Plenty of time." He led me back to bed.

* * *

"This chocolate croissant is heavenly." I savored the richness and bitterness of the dark cacao. "What's your plan for today?"

"Another massage?" Rob grinned and took a big bite of a blueberry pancake—he held his finger up for me to wait. After he swallowed, he said, "Just kidding. I've heard the library here is nice, so I thought I'd finish putting the paper to bed there while you go to your cooking class. What are they teaching today?"

I lifted the listing. "Seafood and knife skills. I need help with both. You could still join me." I nudged his calf with my bare foot.

"I'll go to the one tomorrow on Mediterranean cooking. Need to finish a few things this morning."

I popped the last of the croissant into my mouth, stood, and pointed toward the shower. Rob nodded and turned his attention back to the daily cruise bulletin.

After I finished, Rob and I traded places, and I donned shorts, sandals, and a polo shirt. Before leaving, I opened the bathroom door as he was shaving and blew him a kiss.

We must have hit a rough patch, or the winds shifted because the seas were rockier. I was happy the travel agent had urged Rob to pick a cabin in the middle of the ship because it would have felt far more noticeable on either end. With a light grip on the hallway handrail and then on the stairs, I made my way up to the eleventh floor for the class.

As the participants walked in, we were instructed to wash our hands in the large sink by the door. Then we were given white aprons to protect our clothes and a towel to hook on the tie around our waists. There were three long "L" shaped tables with beige quartz countertops divided by small stainless steel two-burner glass cooktops and tiny sinks. Cameras were positioned around where the chef would be demonstrating to show close-ups of the detailed parts on the large TV monitors hanging from the ceiling over her workspace.

I stood by one of the stations in the front of the room, happy to note a sous chef must have done most of the prep work for us. Each station had four small white ramekins in the front containing different ingredients, along with a scallop on a separate dish. One held sliced garlic, another diced green and red peppers, then minced shallots, and the last appeared to be clarified butter. I bent for a better sniff of the mélange.

The places were filling up fast, and then Dawn Calhoun wandered in, hesitating as she scanned the crowd. She slid into the spot next to me and said, "It's good to see a familiar face."

I was surprised. "I didn't think I'd see you today. How are you doing?"

"As good as could be expected, I guess." Her mouth quivered. "I probably shouldn't be here, but hanging out in our suite was making me crazy." She paused. "I can lose myself when I cook, and I had signed up for this class..." She shrugged.

"Well, I'm glad you did."

The instructor tapped on her microphone. "Welcome to the Cooking Fish course. I hope you'll discover new techniques and maybe try fish you've never had before. Today, we'll be working with a scallop," She held a small dish, "Tilapia," she held up another, "and cod. Let's get started."

"Please scrape the clarified butter into the pan. Does anyone know why we use that?"

Dawn murmured, "Higher smoke point."

"Correct. It will not burn because the milk solids have been removed." A nutty smell filled the room as everyone placed butter into their heated pans. "Now dab the scallop with a paper towel to make sure it's dry and slide it into the pan."

The pan sizzled as I placed the scallop in the hot butter. I nodded at Dawn. "This is going to be yummy."

"Don't turn it till I tell you. We want to get a nice sear." The instructor waited a moment or two. "Now turn it." The scallop had a crisp brown top and, after another minute, she placed it onto a warmed plate. "While that's resting, we'll do a quick sauté of the shallots, peppers, and garlic. Turn the heat to medium. We don't want them to burn." She slid the garnish in and used her spatula as a stirrer. "That's about right, now, take your tongs and delicately array the vegetables on top of the scallop in a nice line."

I studied my effort. It wasn't too bad, although there were probably too many peppers on top of my fish. I turned toward Dawn. Her plate was beautifully adorned with reds and greens in a narrow band across the scallop. "That looks wonderful."

She smiled. "Thanks. I've had practice. After the high stress of my job, cooking relaxes me. Butch hired a chef to train us, and she always said, 'we eat with our eyes first.' I guess she was right."

"What do you do?" I asked.

"Butch's assistant."

The instructor finished inspecting the students' dishes. "You did very well. In a few minutes, we'll move on to poaching salmon in papillote or paper but, for now, sample your efforts as your sous chefs set up for the next dish."

Dawn and I pulled bar stools forward and sat. I cut a sliver of scallop and placed it in my mouth. "This is good."

Dawn nodded. "I'm glad I came. I didn't think I'd be hungry, but I am."

"Sheila mentioned your attorney is on the boat. It must be strange traveling with him."

"You get used to it. One of Butch's quirks—he didn't like a lot of down time." Her eyes misted. "Maybe if he truly had relaxed, he wouldn't have died."

"How long were you married?"

A man cleared the dirty pan and plates from in front of us. "Would you like a coffee or a glass of wine?"

"White for me," Dawn said.

"Coffee, one sugar."

"We were only married two years. It's cliché, but I started out of school, and he swept me off my feet—dinners at expensive restaurants, Broadway shows, that kind of thing. It was special for someone who grew up with not a lot of extras.

"At first, he was so solicitous. That didn't last too long once we were married. He was a thrill seeker, and maybe he was done once the chase was over. And now he's gone." She popped the rest of the scallop into her mouth.

A tall man in his mid-thirties with sea-blue eyes, a chiseled chin, and a body to match wore a dark blue suit and waved through the glass door. The instructor opened it. "Can I help you?

Dawn sighed. "He's looking for me." She rose and nodded. "The lawyer. It was nice to see you again."

Who wears a suit during the day on a Caribbean cruise?

I enjoyed the rest of the class and decided when I got home, I'd branch out from our usual salmon dinners. After chatting with the instructor and getting printed copies of the recipes, I left the class, turned right, and walked down the hall to the library. Double doors opened to a peaceful sanctuary with ebony bookshelves lined with the latest hardcovers. The floor was a dark hard wood set in a herringbone pattern, and evergreen leather wing chairs studded with gold reminded me of an upscale men's club.

The room was larger than it first appeared because it continued around a corner, after which was a wide expanse of a combination of standard bookshelves and squares on a diagonal to display larger coffee table varieties. I continued to the end of the room and found Rob tucked away in a computer kiosk.

I kissed his neck. "This is my idea of heaven."

He pulled me onto his lap. "This is mine."

"Almost done?"

"Ten more minutes?"

"Take your time—I'll browse." I surveyed the stacks, pulled out a new mystery I'd meant to read, and settled into one of the comfy chairs. The book embraced me, and I surrendered to the story. One of the characters was walking through a fell mist on the moors as a shrouded person leaped from behind a boulder. I jumped when I realized someone was standing next to me. It was Randy Calhoun.

"I didn't mean to scare you." He sank onto the chair opposite me.

"The book." I shrugged. "Is there something I can help you with?"

"Not really. I'm just at loose ends. I thought I might find something to read."

I nodded, still trying to figure out why he was talking to me.

"Everything's so crazy now. Lawyers, accountants, and questions from the ship's security people. And Dad. This was supposed to be a fun trip. We'd landed a big new client and were celebrating. Now everything's up in the air, and we're not even sure who gets the company. Apparently, there was a new will back in New York. Our attorney on the ship didn't even know about it." He put his face into his hands. "What a mess."

"Who did you think would get control?" I couldn't help myself. I had to ask.

"Me, of course." His face reddened. "I'm his son, and I did a lot of the work. I even introduced Dad to the new client. It should be me. Instead, it might be her."

"Her? Your sister?"

"Dawn. That ingrate."

Chapter 5

Rob smoothed sunscreen on my back in slow circles. "That's interesting. Dawn might inherit the company. I would have thought they'd have had some kind of prenup."

I shaded my eyes as I turned. "Don't they go away at death—I think it's only used if you get divorced. Besides, not everyone has one. We don't."

"We kind of did. We made arrangements for Jenny."

"And we don't have that kind of money."

He nodded. "And we don't have that kind of age difference."

"She was his assistant. I wonder what her background is. I assumed she was his secretary. Maybe she was far more than that. I may need to let my fingers do some walking."

Rob put the cap onto the lotion and tucked it into the beach bag. Then, he lay back and shut his eyes. "Sun feels great—think I'll nap for a bit."

I opened my book and tried to concentrate on the story. *What was Dawn's background—how much money was Butch's company worth— did Butch's daughter get anything?* I came to the end of the chapter and realized I had no idea what I had just read. Rob's mouth sagged slightly, and his face was slack. He wouldn't notice if I left for a few minutes. I grabbed my phone, slid on my cover-up, and strode through the ship to the library.

Everyone must have been enjoying the sun or doing other things because the room was empty. I slipped into the seat Rob had occupied previously, pulled up the internet, and searched for Dawn Calhoun. Nothing came up, so I searched 'Butch Calhoun.' There were pages of results, but I started with his Wikipedia page. It stated he was born in 1950 and he had started his investment firm, Calhoun Investments, in 1974. His net worth was estimated to be north of twenty billion. I whistled—a lot of money.

I clicked on the personal information tab, and my eyes widened. His first wife, Susan, disappeared in 2005 under mysterious circumstances. They never found her and, after seven years, Butch petitioned the courts to declare her dead. I sat back in the chair. How awful for Randy and Becky to have lost their mother, especially not knowing what happened to her. I checked Randy and Becky's dates of birth. They were twenty and sixteen, respectively, when she left. How sad for them, especially Becky. She was only one year younger than Jenny was now. I shuddered. I couldn't imagine waltzing off and leaving Jenny.

Butch's second wife was listed as Dawn Franklin. I then searched on that name and hit the jackpot. Dawn had graduated from an ivy league school and continued to get her master's degree. Why had she gone to work for Butch as an assistant? Sounded like she did a heck of a lot more than scheduling meetings.

I stretched, attempting to get rid of the stiffness in my lower back when my phone pinged with a message from Rob: "Where are you? I'm ordering a pina colada. Do you want one?"

"Sold. Be right there." I closed the browser and walked back to the pool.

A waiter handed Rob two drinks as I came up behind him. "Perfect timing." I kissed Rob, sat on the chaise, and sipped. "Coconut with a hint of pineapple. Just what the doctor ordered."

"Where did you run off to?" He paused. "Wait. Let me guess. The library."

I laughed. "Service is spotty on my phone, and that room is so nice. Want to know what I found out?" I told him.

"That's a lot of money."

"Uh-huh. What do you think happened to his first wife?"

The alarm on Rob's phone rang. "Still want to try out the virtual reality equipment?"

"Of course." I slid on my navy-blue cover-up, and Rob put on his shirt.

"Are we coming back? We could leave this here to keep our chairs." He held up the beach bag.

I shook my head. "I want to try the trivia challenge after virtual reality."

We trotted down the stairs to the room, half expecting to see it still locked, but the sign-up sheet was in place, and our names were on it. Rob knocked on the door, and no one answered, so we opened it and walked in. The headsets were on stands, with a list of games and how to access them hanging on the wall above.

"What's that wide-screen TV for? With everything going on yesterday, I didn't notice it before." I pointed to the far wall.

He lifted the instructions. "It's a monitor. You can turn it on to see what the other person sees. Or you can use the other headset and choose your own game. It's a shame they weren't using it yesterday." He shook his head. "It's going to take forever if we just use one headset. We can always turn it on if we see something."

"I'll try this one. It's based on *Raiders of the Lost Ark*." I put on the headset and was soon running from the boulder. "Whoa! That's so real. That might get your heart beating." I removed the headset. "Which one are you trying?"

He pointed to the list and donned his headset. Soon his arms were waving, and he ran forward. He lifted the apparatus from his head. "Love it. No snakes, though."

We went through a few more, and I said, "This is the one Dawn described." My hands moved as I navigated the desk. Pretty boring. Just my speed.

"It's strange we can't find the one Butch was viewing. Maybe there's someone we could ask."

There was a knock at the door, and a woman stuck her head in. "Almost done? I'm next."

Rob and I wiped the headsets with sanitizer and told her to have a good time. We exited the room, and I turned to him. "I think Jenny would love that. Maybe you and I should go halves."

"You just don't want me to get full credit. You're afraid I'll be the popular parent." Rob laughed.

"Don't be such a tease." I checked my watch. "We're probably dressed respectably enough to play trivia. What do you think?"

"Let's go."

Teams were being formulated when Rob and I walked into the lounge. It was in the ship's bow with a striking ocean view. Long continuous couches in luxurious cream-colored leather faced the bar with thoughtfully spaced bistro tables. Other seating configurations were set up for conversation or wave-watching. Tiny lights were positioned in the ceiling to create the impression of stars, and a piano's ivories stood ready for tinkling. The game was being set up in the middle of the lounge, facing the bar.

Sam called, "Merry, Rob, join Becky and me."

I hesitated, trying to figure out if I could just ignore them. I was getting kind of tired of the whole family. Rob nudged me and whispered, "We have to."

I plastered a smile on my face and walked to where they had set up. "Thanks for inviting us. We've played a bit at our bar at home, but this is the first time on a cruise ship." I sat next to Becky. "I was so sorry about your father."

"I know it's strange for me to be here, but we've been kind of at loose ends in our cabin, and Sam really likes to play."

Sam leaned toward us. "What are your specialties?"

"Sports and world events," Rob said.

"Anything movies. The older, the better." Becky reached for the bowl of pretzels.

Everyone turned toward me, and I shrugged. "General and insurance?"

The social hostess tapped on the microphone, and it squealed. As she went through the rules—no electronics, keep it fun—I zoned out and surveyed the other players. Some seemed hyper-competitive, leaning forward in their seats, and others were using the game as an excuse to party, ordering more drinks from the servers.

Then she said, "Don't forget your answer sheets, one per group, and a pencil. I'll give you a few minutes to get ready." She kept her question page with the answers close to her chest.

There was a scrum as the alpha from each group scurried to the piano to claim their page, triumphant heroes upon their return.

"Everyone ready? There'll be ten questions—please discuss potential answers with your group and then write the final answer in the space provided." The sheet was numbered one through ten, with an underlined blank spot for the answer.

"Remember, the winning team collects points! If you read your cruise newsletter every evening, you'll see it highlights all the great games going on during the day that are eligible for additional points. And at the end of the cruise, you can turn in those points for fun logoed Serendipity of the Seas items."

Sam leaned forward, clutching the pencil, ready for the first question.

"Which animal can be seen on the Porsche logo?"

I shrugged. Becky gestured us all closer and whispered, "Horse. I have one."

"A horse?" Rob queried.

She laughed. "No, a Porsche."

Sam wrote the answer.

Other groups were still working on theirs.

"First woman to win a Nobel Prize?"

"Oh, I know that. She died from radiation poisoning. What was her name?" I frowned.

Rob whispered. "Marie Curie."

Sam scribbled it in.

A group to our left laughed loudly. It seemed they were talking about a lot more than trivia. Then a woman in a group on our right snuck a peek at her phone. I sat up straighter, staring at her. One of her companions touched her arm and gave her a meaningful look, and she slid the phone back into her purse.

Sam got the next tough ones after discussion, and the last question was about the Caribbean. "Which island has the world's oldest rum distillery?"

"Gotta be Barbados," Rob murmured.

Sam said, "I think it's Jamaica. I've been on a rum tour there. Love the spices."

They turned to Becky and me. I shrugged, and Becky echoed.

"I have the pencil. Going with Jamaica. Sorry, Rob."

"No problem." He sat back in his chair.

The social hostess said, "Time to wrap up. I know we have a few folks who still want to be able to get to tea before it ends. And I have it on good authority there are delicious cupcakes available." She smiled. "Now, please exchange your answer sheet with another team."

After waiting a minute for the flurry of activity to die down, she gave the answers. When she got to the one about rum and announced the correct response was Barbados, Sam turned to Rob and mouthed, "Sorry."

We had gotten six correct, but several other groups had gotten more, and one group got all ten answers.

Rob and I stood, and Becky asked, "Are you going to the tea?"

I shook my head. "Been eating a bit too much lately."

"Then stay and have a drink with us. I don't want to go back to the cabin yet, and I'll feel like we should if it's just Sam and me."

Rob and I exchanged glances and then sat back down. I said, "Just one. We'll need to shower and change soon."

Becky smiled. "Thanks."

A waiter stopped at our table, and we gave him our drink order. After he left, Rob turned to Sam. "I know you have a gallery and that Becky exhibits in it—what types of art do you focus on? And how did you get started?"

"I've always loved art. During my gap year, I traveled to Italy and toured the museums, Uffizi Gallery, Palazzo Pitti, and the Accademia Gallery. Don't even get me started on the David. Michelangelo was a wonder. Oh, and the Sistine Chapel in Rome." Sam did a pretend swoon. "So beautiful.

"I came back to the United States and went to school. Unfortunately, I don't have any talent when it comes to creating art, but I do have a good head for business and a great sense for identifying talent." Sam lifted Becky's left hand and kissed it. A large solitaire refracted the light.

"Is that new?" I leaned forward.

Becky nodded and held out her hand. "Sam gave it to me last night. Isn't it beautiful?"

"It's stunning. Congratulations to you both." I smiled, and Rob echoed my sentiment.

"Would have been much sooner, but Butch said he would make Becky's life a living hell if we got engaged. I'm sorry for Becky's sake that he's dead, but you won't find me shedding any tears." Sam sipped her chardonnay.

"Sam!" Becky chided.

"True. Not going to pretend now."

I shifted in my seat, uncomfortable with the tension at the table. Rob asked, "When's the big day?"

"Haven't gotten that far yet. I was lucky the jeweler on board does such quick work," Sam said.

"You didn't have the ring?" I asked.

Sam shook her head. "Thought I would use the time on the ship to convince Butch that Becky and I were made for each other. Then when he died, I figured we didn't need to wait any longer."

Chapter 6

Rob and I returned from the show after dinner. We kicked off our shoes and walked out onto the balcony, quiet for a moment, watching the full moon flick light onto the inky-black sea. I sighed and leaned against him, "What a fun show, and dinner was terrific. That sea bass melted in my mouth. And the basmati rice. So tender."

He kissed the top of my head and put his arms around me. "I'm glad you had a good time. Want to sit here?"

I nodded and sank onto the cushioned rattan chair. He sat beside me and said, "That cruise director has a great set of pipes."

"Sure does. And those songs...so romantic."

He held my hand. "It was nice. Want something to drink?"

I shook my head. "Let's just enjoy the night. The Bailey's at the show was enough for me." The waves rhythmically lapped the boat as the ship plowed through the ocean. "Pull the bed out here—this is so relaxing."

"Might be a tad embarrassing." He winked.

I grinned. "Talk about something else, or I'm going to have to pull you inside and ravish you."

"Would that be so bad?" Rob teased.

"What did you think about what Becky and Sam said?"

"Changing the subject...I see what you're doing." He kissed my nose and then cleared his throat. "I found it interesting they put off their engagement just because Butch wanted them to. Becky's in her early thirties, an adult. Why would she still be listening to him?"

"Other than filial love, the only thing I can think of is money."

"Which gives them a motive." Rob nodded.

A Black-capped Petrel dove into the ocean for a snack. "I didn't think birds were this far out to sea."

"Some spend most of their time here. We must be entering the Caribbean, or that bird is really far from home."

"You know a lot about everything," I quipped.

"Calling me a know-it-all?"

"Not what I said. And now, husband of mine, it's time for bed."

* * *

I stretched in front of the door, musing at the now turquoise water. It would be our last sea day before we started touring, and I planned to make the most of relaxing. Mysterious islands flirted with the horizon, hinting at beautiful secrets waiting to be explored.

The envelope containing tour tickets was on the desk, almost within reach. I extended my arm. *A little more.* My fingertips grazed it, and I was able to bat it to the floor. I pulled out the top ticket for Sandschelle, the cruise line's private island. We were going to visit a butterfly farm, a place where they grew aloe, and a beach where the snorkeling was supposed to be wonderful. That would be fun. My eyes grew wide when I saw the departure time. We needed to be in the theater at seven forty-five—in the morning—while we were on vacation. I sighed. At home, I would have been up and dressed earlier than that. Then, I chuckled when I realized I had gotten too used to being a lady of leisure.

The suite door opened, and Rob walked in, balancing two cups.

"Is that what I think it is?"

"Cappuccino for the beautiful bride." He put one on the desk, and I stood.

"Thank you." I kissed him. "What time did you get up? I didn't hear you leave."

41

"Seven. You were sleeping so peacefully I didn't want to disturb you."

I sipped the magic elixir. "Just right. Any thoughts on what we ought to do today?"

"Breakfast. Then lazing by the pool. There's a putting tourney at eleven that might be fun."

"Sounds like you've given this a lot of thought."

He lifted my chin and kissed me. "Loads. Let's do the breakfast buffet. I'm hungry."

I slid on my sandals, grabbed my key, and we walked out the door and climbed the stairs to the restaurant. I scanned the menu in the foyer and asked Rob, "Outside?"

He nodded. I led the way through the more casual restaurant, past full tables of convivial diners all the way to the back of the ship, and found a table for two in the shade. The sun was bright, and the air warm enough to make it a delightful morning to eat and relax under an umbrella. Fish cavorted in the engines' wake, and birds, hungry for a meal, dove after them.

"Coffee?" A waiter approached with a pot. I nodded, and he poured.

Rob shook his head. "Mimosa for me. And water."

"Ooh. That sounds good. For me too."

I put my sunglasses on the top of the table, and Rob and I walked inside to the buffet. I took a small bowl and added fresh strawberries and blueberries with a dollop of yogurt. Then I wandered by the grill. The specialty that morning was french toast and caramelized bananas. *I really shouldn't.* I shrugged. *Tomorrow, I'll be good.* I gave the server my table number.

Rob raised an eyebrow when I returned to the table. "That's all you're having?" He pointed to his plate piled high with scrambled eggs, crispy potatoes, beans, and sausages.

I smiled. "Ordered the special from the grill. I'll have a sugar high through dinner." I sat and started on my yogurt.

Dawn and the lawyer were sitting on the other side of the deck in deep discussion—fluttering paperwork weighed down by various glasses and silverware. He had modified his wardrobe and was now in lime green shorts and a yellow polo shirt. I poked Rob's arm, motioned him closer, and pointed toward the two. "Last time I saw him, he was wearing a suit. Guess the new boss isn't as concerned about appearances."

Randy stalked onto the deck and confronted the duo. "Don't think I don't know what's going on. They said Dad died of natural causes. A heart attack. Hah! I know you had something to do with it. When I think of all the times I defended you, held your hand when Dad was on a tear... I'm going to fight this. You won't get this company if it's the last thing I do."

Two waiters approached and spoke with him. Dawn's face was ashen, and she was grinding her teeth. The lawyer squirmed as if he was caught with his hand in the cookie jar.

"I won't calm down. She killed my father. I know it," Randy shouted.

The waiters continued to talk with him in low tones.

Finally, he hung his head. "All right. I'll leave." He walked out between the two waiters.

The Maître D' arrived and spoke with Dawn and the lawyer. She had regained color and shook her head at something he said, and he retreated.

Conversations resumed at the various tables, and I turned to Rob. "What was that all about?"

"I guess they decided he died of a heart attack. From what Sheila said, he had a bad ticker."

"But that snake you saw—"

"I know. Randy may not be wrong. There's something fishy about how it suddenly disappeared."

"What should we do?" My french toast arrived and I played with it, suddenly not hungry. I speared a caramelized banana.

"Not much we can do. I tried to show the security guy what was on the headset, but it was gone. Plus, we're on our honeymoon. This is one investigation we don't need to be involved in."

I groaned. "But what if—"

"Merry, they'll work it out." Rob signaled to the waiter for another mimosa. I covered my glass with my hand.

The rest of breakfast was uneventful, and then we decided to drop by a lecture on underwater wonders by a naturalist the cruise liner had brought on board. His presentation was fascinating, and afterward, Rob and I moved into the sea of people exiting the theater.

I wrapped my arm around Rob's waist. "Do you think we'll see sharks on this trip?"

"Hopefully not."

"But they're so graceful. Them and the stingrays. Oh, and the sea anemones. Their tentacles and colors are mesmerizing." I waved my hand to mimic their movement. "I hope we see those."

Rob put his arm around my shoulders. "I think someone's getting excited to get off the boat."

"You could be correct." I chuckled. "What's next on the agenda?"

"Putting tourney?"

"Why not." We hurried to the top deck behind the stacks and arrived just as the assistant cruise director handed out clubs. The course wasn't big, only nine narrow holes that took up much of the ship's stern above the restaurant we had been in for breakfast. The small space was fairly crowded with people wanting to play, so Rob told him, "We can share one."

Sam came up on the other side of Rob and laughed. "It might be better if Merry and I share one. Your back will go out if you get one short enough for her."

He selected a longer club and turned to Sam. "My back thanks you."

"Where's Becky?" I asked.

"Family meeting. Some hubbub about what will happen when we dock tomorrow. The cruise company says the island isn't big enough to have the facilities to take Butch off. Randy wants them to investigate and use the island police, but they're not big enough either. It's kind of a mess." She gave a rueful smile and shrugged.

"It is pretty tiny. I guess some people live on the island full time, but it's mostly scrub, aloe, and beach." Rob frowned. "Plus, didn't I hear the doctor said he died of natural causes? Why would they need police?"

"How'd you hear that already? We just found out today." Sam put her red ball on the mat and eyed the hole hiding behind an elevated green triangle.

"Randy was upset and shouted at Dawn this morning," I explained.

Sam banked the shot against the right wall, setting herself up for an easy shot on her next turn. "Randy and Dawn seemed thick as thieves before, and then Butch dies and wham. Hate each other's guts. Becky's taken to calling Dawn the "Black Widow," after that late-eighties film where the woman marries then kills all the men for their money."

"You think Dawn had something to do with Butch's death?" Rob placed his ball on the mat.

"She seemed nice enough to me. He was a tough cookie, and I had a lot of sympathy for what he put her through. But now, seems like she made the right bet." Sam handed me the putter.

"How so?" Rob's ball careened off the raised grass and landed in no man's land.

I muttered, "Bad luck," and teed up my shot.

"She gets control over the firm, the family houses, and mega bucks for a few short years with the guy. Not what I'd want to do, but I guess she played it right."

"What about Becky?" We moved to the next hole.

"She wasn't part of the company, so she had no expectation along that line. Butch left her money separately."

We continued the game, and Rob rallied to come in second while Sam took first. She and Rob collected their points from the assistant cruise director while I nursed my injured pride, having come in ninth. Sam waved to me as she left.

On his return, Rob kissed my forehead. "I'll share the points with you."

"No sympathy winnings for me." I shook my head. "Wait till trivia today. Maybe we should be on separate teams."

He took a step back and clutched his chest. "Separating already?"

"Silly. C'mon, let's go to the pool."

We walked down the stairs to the pool deck and squeezed past a few occupied chairs to ones in the middle. I sank onto the nearer one and arranged the towel to my liking. "Need some time to relax after that strenuous exercise."

Rob handed me my book and the sunscreen. "Better reapply."

I lathered up. "I am getting kind of excited about getting off the boat tomorrow. Do you think they'll have souvenirs? I haven't gotten anything for Jenny yet."

"Company-owned island. They'll have merchandise." He tipped his ball cap to cover his face.

✳ ✳ ✳

I stood in line the following day behind all the other caffeine addicts and grumbled. "Why do we have to leave so early?"

Rob flipped the lever for the urn, and magic elixir poured into my to-go cup. Then he filled his own. "First, it's Thanksgiving, so if we were home, we would have been up early to put the turkey in the oven. Second, if we're the first group out, we'll get dibs on the chairs at the beach. And even more important, the snorkel equipment."

"Thanks for reminding me. Patty told me to call around four—she figured that would be between dinner and dessert. I wish the Wi-Fi were better. I could do a video chat." I sighed and turned toward the theater, coffee in hand. Long midnight-blue, padded benches made arched rows on the floor, bisecting the aisles running toward the stage. Intimate tables stood in front of them, perfect for holding beverages during shows. Alternating with the benches were navy chairs with silver stars. I sank onto one of them and sipped coffee. "Might need a second."

Rob chuckled as he sat next to me.

One of the destination crew announced, "If you're in the seven forty-five group, please turn in your tour vouchers for tickets—we'll be leaving shortly."

I handed him the papers, and he exchanged them with the crew for numbered plastic tags. We joined the line of people leaving the theater and walked down the stairs to the tender station. Two of the crew were stationed on either side of the opening to hand people to a waiting crew member inside the shuttle boat. Rob went first as the ship and the smaller boat were not rising and falling in unison. One of the topside crew said, "Now," and Rob stepped forward onto the tender. I relayed my coffee through the crew to Rob and followed. "That went smoothly."

"They have a lot of practice." Rob intertwined his fingers with mine, and we moved forward to two seats near the door on the other side.

The boat was almost full, and then Randy and Sheila were handed down. Sheila pointed toward the two seats near us, and they sat. "We almost didn't make it. I read the time wrong." She turned her face into the breeze, and her hair fluttered. "It's going to be great to get off the ship for a day."

I nodded as I gritted my teeth. It was wrong, but I wondered if somehow this family was dogging us. *Maybe they're not on the same tour. We could get lucky.* I shifted slightly so I could see the tags Randy was holding. *Darn it.* They were the same as Rob's.

The boat moved away from the ship and made a large loop before heading for the dock, and then a crew member met us as we disembarked. She pointed toward a waiting bus, and we formed an obedient line, handing the tags to the tour operator as we boarded. Randy and Sheila sat across from us.

The bus jerked forward, and Rob said, "Ow," as his knees were crushed against the seat in front of us. Being height challenged, I had plenty of room.

"Turn sideways—it might be better."

He complied. "This way, I'll only lose one knee cap."

"I don't think they're used to taller Americans." I hugged Rob's arm. "That beach is gorgeous. Hopefully, it's where we'll be headed later." A snow-white expanse of sand dotted by red and blue padded chaise lounges trailed into the azure sea.

"Hopefully, the drive isn't long."

Pine trees dotted the otherwise barren landscape, and small multi-hued wooden huts began to appear. Sheila reached across the aisle to poke Rob's arm. "Why are there evergreens here? I just thought they'd be up north."

The tour guide broke in. "You'll note the forested area off to our right. Evergreens were planted as an experiment after the last hurricane because they have a much deeper root system than palms. You can see for yourself how they've thrived. You'll also see small huts that house the seasonal workers.

"Now, our first stop is at a small aloe farm. There you'll see the different uses of aloe in the products made here on the island and will have a few moments in the gift shop, should you wish to take home souvenirs."

"That'd be perfect for Jenny and Patty," I said.

Rob chuckled. "Why do I think this will be an expensive day?"

The bus slowed to a stop in front of the aloe farm. A woman waited for us under the shade of a palapa, a large wooden table in front of her with a beige bucket on top, several aloe plants, and a large knife. The rustic gift shop stood behind her.

We gathered around as she explained. "I'm going to cut near the base of the aloe plant—note I'm choosing a nice thick leaf." She cut. "Now I'm going to slice all along the periphery. You see this yellow stuff?" She exposed the inside. "That's called aloin. You don't want to eat that—it'll make you spend a lot of unpleasant time in the bathroom."

Randy muttered, "Wish I had some for Dawn."

"You can't be serious." My mouth dropped.

"Kidding. Of course, I'm kidding." He held up both hands in protest.

We turned back to the demonstration as the woman continued. "Now I want to rinse it to make sure all the aloin is gone." She used the bucket for that and then passed the opened leaf to Rob, who was on her left. "Touch the aloe—see how slimy it is?" He complied and then handed it to me, I passed it to Randy, and it made the rounds to the other people on the tour, eventually winding up back with the instructor. "I hope you've enjoyed the demonstration. If you'd like some of the aloe products we make, you'll find them in the gift shop behind me."

The group clapped.

"Want to go in?" I smiled at Rob.

He shook his head. "Have fun. I'm going to explore the fields."

"I'll join you," Randy said.

Sheila linked arms with me. "We can go together."

I sighed as I allowed myself to be led to the store.

Glass shelves lined all four walls, taking advantage of every inch of the small store. Despite the rustic outside, it was relatively modern and antiseptic, like something in an upscale department store back home. Painted in soothing tones of green, it played off the color of the plants outside. There were foot creams, pain ointments, face treatments, and moisturizers. Sheila seemed determined to try all the testers. I zeroed in on the one for the foot cream—it had a light fragrance—floral with an undertone of mint. I picked up two, one for Patty and the other for Jenny, and walked toward the register. *Who am I kidding?* I scurried

49

back and retrieved one for myself. Then I saw shaving gel. That would be nice for Rob. I tucked it into the basket.

The woman at the register asked, "Did you see our lip balm? It'll be the perfect thing for when you have to face those winters up north. It has a nice lemony scent, and it's two dollars off with your purchase." I retrieved three from the display, and she added them to the bill.

I paid and turned to leave. Sheila was behind me with a large basketful of items. I said, "You must have a lot of people to buy for."

"Don't be silly. They're for me, of course." She edged past and dropped the carrier on the counter. "Throw in a few of those lip balms as well."

I held off on the eye roll and said, "See you outside."

She flicked her wrist, and I walked out the door. Rob and Randy were leaning against the palapa, and Rob eyed my bag and said, "I was expecting something larger."

"Good things come in small packages." I laughed.

The tour operator was motioning people toward the bus, so Rob and I walked that way, leaving Randy to wait for Sheila. Rob whispered, "I peeked in the store to see how much longer you would be, and when I turned, Randy seemed really guilty."

"How so?"

"Hard to describe. Like a kid who knows he did something wrong but thinks he got away with it. Guilty, yet a little smug."

I clambered onto the bus with Rob behind me. He lifted my package to the rack above our seats, and we sat. I turned to him. "Weird."

"Strange guy." Rob shrugged.

The butterfly farm was lovely, with all different types cavorting around the fresh-fruit buffet artfully arrayed for them. One with iridescent blue markings against a velvety black background landed on Rob's shoulder, and I took a picture with my phone. "Such a beautiful color."

The guide showed us a shadow box with various chrysalises hanging from pegs. He explained they were at different stages of hatching and, as we studied it, a butterfly began to emerge from one. After the presentation portion, we wandered the farm, enjoying the trail and the various fountains that dominated ponds throughout.

Unfortunately, all too soon, the tour guide advised we needed to get back on the bus. As we slid onto our seats, Rob said, "Not going to lie; I'm happy this is the last time we'll be on this coach. It'll be good to stretch my legs and relax when we get to the beach."

"Poor baby." I rubbed his shoulder.

Randy and Sheila sat, and he said, "They aren't generous with the leg room, are they?" Randy and Sheila's knees were pressed against the seat in front of them.

"Can't wait to get to the beach." Rob nodded.

The bus left the parking lot, and a few minutes later, the turquoise sea dashed white against the dark brown rocks on the left side of the bus. Further out, the color changed to navy blue, and the barren coast with anemic scrub gave way to lush trees and a picture-perfect protected cove replete with pearly-white sand. The bus pulled into the parking lot, and the tour guide said, "Check around your seat and above it to ensure you have all your belongings. There are lockers on your right—remember to take the key with you."

We hopped off, and I went to the area she had described. Rob lifted the bag with my purchases into the locker and closed the door. "I'm glad they have the key attached to this flexible wristband. I'd be worried I'd lose it."

I kicked off my sneakers and dug my toes in the sand. "So soft."

Rob grabbed my hand, and we wound our way past the sea of chairs to the two nearest the ocean and a little apart from the others with a small table in between. As I sat, a man handed each of us a towel. "Would you like something to drink? A soda, or a Bloody Mary, perhaps?"

51

"Club soda with lime, please," I replied.

"Bloody Mary for me." Rob smacked his lips.

I leaned back onto the chaise lounge and shut my eyes. "So peaceful." The gently breaking waves, cries of seagulls searching for lunch, and sweet aroma of salt from the sea breeze were relaxing.

Something was being dragged through the sand. I shaded my eyes and turned. Randy was moving the chaises for him and Sheila to our secluded area. "Hope you don't mind, but this is a better spot."

"Fine," Rob grunted.

The server put our drinks on the table, handed Randy and Sheila towels, and they ordered.

"Such a beautiful spot," Sheila said. "I just love the beach."

I murmured, "Uh-huh," and shut my eyes, praying she'd be quiet.

"You're not sleepy, are you?" She tapped my shoulder.

"A little."

"Well, don't mind me. I can just read a book or watch the waves." She sat up straight. "Ooh. There's a dolphin—and he must have some sisters and brothers."

I put my sunglasses on and watched the mammals cavort.

A waiter walked by, offering cold fruit skewers. Sheila waved him toward us, and we all took one. She laughed, "With all I've been eating, I'm sure to gain thirty pounds." She put her hand on her hip and struck a pose, giving lie to that statement.

"You look great."

"It's tough out there. You top thirty, and it's harder to get men to pant over you. And somehow, the more powerful they are, the more attractive young women they hire. Like the ones in Butch's office. They're always on the prowl. Though with Dawn at the helm, that's sure to stop." She plucked a pineapple from the skewer and tossed it in her mouth. "I probably won't have to worry as much now, though, with Randy no longer in line for succession. And if he keeps alienating Dawn, who knows how much longer he'll be there."

Randy gave her a scathing glance and dragged his chair to the other side of Rob. They began to discuss the football season.

I gave a silent groan, knowing this conversation would continue no matter how much I craved solitude. "Did you ever think about going to work? Maybe then you wouldn't worry as much."

"I did plenty of that before I married Randy. Still keep my hand in the game to keep my skills up and earn pin money." She leaned closer. "Becky sure got a sweet deal. Money outright, no business ties, and now she can marry Sam. If I didn't know he died a natural death, I'd say she had something to do with it."

Chapter 7

I pulled the wand from the mascara tube and applied it to my lashes. "All I wanted to do was sleep on the beach. And that woman kept talking and talking. I thought she was never going to stop. At least I had my call with Jenny. Texting is good for short messages, but nothing takes the place of hearing her voice. Although I was a little concerned about Drew's new venture—whatever that is. We know that's never good." I slipped my feet into a pair of black high heels.

Rob shrugged into his sport coat. "All I can say is I'm glad we have a reservation for two at Pan-Asia. As much as the Calhoun family dynamic interests me, I'm excited about some alone time with you."

"Me too." I lifted my cheek toward him for a kiss.

We exited the suite and took the stairs up one flight. The hostess brought us to a romantic spot for two against the windows with plush chartreuse chairs, a round table with starched white linens, and an overlarge pendant light that included a black lamp shade with dark pagodas inside against a cream background. It was almost over-the-top opulent. We ordered warmed sake, and Rob surveyed the menu. "Lobster tempura. And sushi to start. What are you thinking of ordering?"

Dawn strolled to the hostess station, and I lifted my menu higher. I would have ducked if I hadn't thought I'd seem silly. As she passed our table, she stopped. "Hello, Merry, Rob. I'm all alone this evening. Would you mind if I joined you?"

"We'd love that, but it's a table for two." I put the menu down.

"Can they be moved to one of those tables?" Dawn asked the hostess as she pointed to the middle of the restaurant. "Or are they already spoken for?"

I said a silent prayer.

"That's not a problem, Ms. Franklin." She snapped her fingers at one of the waiters, "Please move this party to table number twelve."

I guess when you're in one of the really expensive suites, they'll accommodate anything you want. I bit the inside of my cheek and gave myself a silent pep talk as Rob and I stood and marched to the new table. Dawn sat, and the hostess handed her a menu. Dawn said, "I'm so glad you haven't ordered yet."

"Us too." Rob was apparently searching for a smile and only ended up halfway there.

The waiter poured wine while Dawn and I studied the menu. I asked her, "What are you getting?"

"I had canapes with Randy and Sheila, so I'll try the miso soup."

"Forgive me, but when we were at breakfast yesterday, it didn't seem like you were getting along." Rob folded his menu.

"Bump in the road. He was surprised I got control of the company. He still owns forty percent, so we need to be at least cordial. We were friends before his father's death, and I have no doubt he'll come around once he realizes his father made the right decision." Dawn sipped the wine. "This is nice."

I asked. "Pardon me for asking, but it seems like people were surprised by the will. Were you?"

"I had no idea Butch's will was so widely discussed." She paused.

I could feel my face get hotter, but then I figured if she was going to interrupt our dinner, payment would be me getting my curiosity satisfied.

She shrugged. "We had discussed it off and on. I wasn't a hundred percent certain he had changed it, but I'm glad he did."

The waiter came, and we ordered.

"I've been on the phone with clients, assuring them they will still be our number one priority. Luckily, I was in most meetings with Butch, so they know me." Dawn smiled. "I can't wait for this meal. I've heard good things about this restaurant."

Our starters came. I had opted for pot stickers, which were light, fluffy, delicious dumplings with a side drizzle of black rice vinegar. I gave Rob one of my dumplings for a salmon-avocado roll. Dawn declined one of ours and focused on her soup.

"Dawn, are you okay?" I leaned toward her because she had suddenly gone ghostly pale.

She clutched her stomach. "Not feeling too well." She jumped to her feet and ran out of the restaurant.

Rob and I stared at each other, and then I said, "I'll be back in a moment." I followed Dawn to the ladies' room, where she was being quite sick in one of the stalls. I eased back out the door and went to the hostess station. "Ms. Franklin is ill in the restroom. You may want to call the doctor."

The hostess said, "I hope she's not allergic to seafood. She scanned her list. "It doesn't say so here."

"Check later. Call the doctor now."

She jerked. "Right away."

I walked back to the restroom and said, "Dawn, are you all right? They're calling the doctor."

"I'm sick."

The doctor knocked and rushed in.

I pointed to a stall. "She's in there."

"Ms. Franklin?" He knocked and then said to me, "You can leave now. Thanks for alerting us."

I left but was unsure what to do. It felt like I should call someone, but with their family at odds... I walked to the house phone, called Randy's room, and he answered, "Yes?"

"It's Merry March. I'm afraid Dawn is ill. The doctor's with her now, but I thought I should tell somebody."

"Thanks for letting me know." Before he hung up, I thought I heard him laugh.

I walked back to the table, and Rob asked, "Is she okay?"

"Some kind of stomach issue." I sat and noted the cleared table. "I hadn't finished. Why didn't you—"

"They took our starters back and said they'd give us new ones when you returned."

A waiter delivered our redone appetizers.

I sipped sake. "Not the way I wanted to be eating alone tonight. I'll call the doctor for an update when we get back to the room."

✻ ✻ ✻

When we returned to the suite after dinner and a musical show, I lifted the phone and pressed the button for medical. "Hello, this is Merry March. I was with Dawn Franklin this evening, and I wanted to check on her."

A deep baritone I recognized as belonging to the doctor replied. "She's doing much better now and should be able to return to her suite in the morning."

"Thank you, Doctor." I hung up. "One less thing to worry about. Dawn is doing better."

"Good. Ready for bed?"

I cuddled against him, and he put his arm around me. I said, "It was the strangest thing. I could have sworn I heard Randy laugh after I told him Dawn was ailing."

He murmured into my hair, "It was weird he invited her for cocktails with all the bad blood between them. You don't think he slipped her anything, do you?"

"What was that yellow stuff from the aloe plant the woman who was demonstrating said was bad for you?" I asked.

"Aloin?"

I lifted my phone from the bedside table, typed "Aloin" into the search engine, and waited for what seemed like a minute or two because of the slow service in the cabin. "Causes stomach distress." I paused, deep in thought. "All those packages Sheila bought. What if...no. They wouldn't want to make customers ill." I turned and propped myself up on my elbow. "Didn't you say Randy looked guilty at some point? When was that?"

Rob frowned. "At the aloe place. I poked my head in the door to see how much longer you and—"

"Where was Randy?"

"By the plants."

I gasped. "You don't think he smuggled one on board?"

* * *

We weren't docking till later in Bonaire, so Rob and I decided to have breakfast on our balcony. He opted for a bagel and fruit, and I ordered blueberry pancakes. "I'm going to have to go on a diet when I get home because my pants are getting a little tight."

Rob kissed my cheek. "Perfect, just the way you are. Don't get as neurotic about food as my mother, or I'll have to leave you."

"Not going that far." I laughed. "Still plan on enjoying all life offers, maybe just at a more moderate pace."

"What time do we leave?"

I lifted the tour ticket. "Says to be in the theater at eleven-thirty."

"We have a few hours—what's your plan?"

"First, I want to check on Dawn." I showed Rob the activity sheet for the day. "Then we can learn bridge..."

"Pass."

"Needlepoint?"

"Hard pass."

"Or play Baggo."

"Ding, ding, ding, the lady has a winner." He laughed. "Let's go find Dawn."

The operator transferred me to Dawn's room, and she answered, "Hello?"

"Dawn, it's Merry March. Rob and I wanted to stop by to see you, but we don't have your room number."

"Give me a few minutes, but we're...I'm on the fourteenth floor all the way at the end. The Grandeur Suite."

I pressed end and turned toward Rob. "The Grandeur Suite. Fancy-dancy. What's our plan?"

"I thought we were checking on her."

"Are we going to tell her our suspicions about Randy?"

"Should we get involved? We don't know anything really. And if they've patched things over, I don't want to get everything stirred up."

I stared at him. "What if he tries again? We have to tell her, so she'll be on guard."

"This is going to be uncomfortable, but you're right." He started toward the door.

"I'll take the lead."

"Since we have a few moments, let's stop by the library on eleven and pick up the crossword and Mensa quiz they mentioned in the newsletter. I want to try my hand."

We walked up the stairs. "We are getting a little bit of exercise." Rob laughed and opened the library door. He headed straight for the puzzle section and pulled out two while I browsed the mystery section, trying to catch my breath. I lifted one with an exciting cover to read the jacket.

He stared at the book, then at me.

"Can't ever have too much to read."

"True. Do you think we've given her enough time?"

I nodded, and we jogged the last three flights. At the end of the short corridor were massive mahogany double doors. "I guess this is it." I pressed the bell.

Dawn opened the door, seeming better than she had the night before but still on the lighter side of her ordinarily pale complexion. "I'm so embarrassed. I have no idea what happened." She turned and walked toward a series of large windows with a one-eighty-degree view of the front of the ship.

My mouth dropped as I followed. "This is beautiful."

"I guess it is." She shrugged.

The floors were marble, and a gleaming black baby grand piano provided decoration for the open room on the right. Past that was a full living room and bar, and straight ahead, a table that could seat twelve.

"Want to see outside?"

"If you don't mind." I followed her.

As we traversed toward the balcony, she pointed left and then right. "Those are the bedrooms. She pushed the door to the balcony open. Two large chaises built for two faced the ocean, and just past them was a hot tub for four. "You have quite the setup," Rob said.

"If you don't mind, I'd like to sit out here—the breeze feels good, and I'm still a little queasy. I'm going to have ginger tea. Is there anything you'd like?" She sat on one of the chaises.

"I can get it—I don't want you to have to get up. You're still recovering," I said.

"The butler will do it." She lifted the phone.

Rob said, "A lemonade for me."

"Two."

She gave the order and then put the phone down. "Should be here shortly. Again, I wanted to apologize for last night. Barged in on your dinner and then—"

"If you don't mind me asking, what did you eat when you were with Randy? Are you allergic to any foods?" I interrupted as I perched on the other chaise, and Rob stretched out next to me.

She shook her head. "The doctor went through all that. I had sushi— must have been a bad piece of fish. Strange though—they're so careful about food safety here."

"Did you see the waiter bring the tray into Randy's suite?"

"It was there when I arrived." Her eyebrow rose. "What are you implying?"

"Nothing." Rob shook his head. "Just trying to understand what happened."

The doorbell rang, and the butler appeared at the glass door a moment later. He opened it and slid the drinks onto the table, along with a plate of cookies. "I thought you might like ginger snaps. Will there be anything else?"

Dawn shook her head, and he withdrew.

I handed Rob one of the lemonades and a cookie. "Did the fish taste off?"

"Not that I recall. Maybe a tad bitter? To be honest, I eat sushi with wasabi, so it would have been kind of tough to tell." She gave a rueful chuckle. "Maybe my lesson is to taste first and then garnish."

"But you're feeling better now?" Rob queried.

Dawn blew on the tea and nodded. "Won't be an adventurous eater for a bit, but I was able to keep brioche toast and a soft-boiled egg down this morning." She sipped and then turned toward me. "I appreciate your concern but don't want to intrude on your time on the ship."

Rob started to stand, but I pulled on his arm and said, "Dawn, we did want to check on you, but we're also here to warn you."

"Me? Why?"

"Randy may have done something—may have put something in your food."

"That's absurd. I know we haven't been getting along lately, but he wouldn't do that. You really think he would want to harm me?" Dawn shook her head. "I can't see it. What makes you say that?"

"We don't know for sure," Rob explained what happened on the island.

Dawn frowned. "A lot of supposition."

"We agree. But, just in case, we wanted to tell you," I said.

The lawyer opened the door. "I'm sorry, Dawn. Is this a bad time?"

Rob and I stood, and he said, "We were just leaving."

"This is my lawyer, Michael Grant. Michael, this is Merry March and her husband, Rob Jenson," Dawn said.

"Pleased to meet you." He shook our hands and then turned to Dawn. "Out here or inside?"

She eyed the papers in his hand and sighed. "Inside. Those will blow all over the place out here." She took her teacup with her and accompanied us to the door. "Thank you for checking on me. I appreciate the warning, but I'm sure it was just the miso soup or a bad piece of fish."

Rob and I left her suite and wandered to the pool deck, where a staff member signed people up for the cornhole game. Rob wrote our names, and we sat on nearby chaises to wait. A few minutes later, Sam and Becky arrived and came toward us. Sam said to Rob, "Ready to be beaten again?"

He laughed. "Don't tell me you're as good at this as at mini golf?"

"Better," Becky said as she slipped her arm around Sam. "My fiancée is all around wonderful."

Sam blushed. "Just athletic."

"Can I ask you a question?" I crossed my legs and leaned back on the lounge chair.

Sam pointed to herself and then to Becky. "Which one of us?"

"Either."

"Shoot." Becky pulled up a chaise, sat, and patted the space next to her for Sam.

"We just met Michael Grant, and he seems fairly young to be Butch's attorney. I would've thought he'd have picked someone nearer his age."

"He did. Michael's father heads up the firm Butch chose, and he was a close friend. He had a hip replacement, and the doctor didn't want him to travel, so Michael came instead. He's thirty-five, just two years older than me. Nice guy, but a bit of a climber." Becky leaned against Sam.

"How so?" Rob stood as the staff member called our names.

"It wouldn't surprise me if he and the merry widow end up together," Sam said.

We took the bags handed to us as the staff person explained the rules. I balanced one and whispered to Rob, "When the butler came, he rang the bell. Michael just appeared at the balcony door. Does he have a key? Or was he already in the suite? Did they seem close to you?"

He shook his head as he lobbed one and missed. It landed just left of the board on the deck. "Quiet now. I need to concentrate."

✳ ✳ ✳

Patty, Jenny, and my assistant, Cheryl, texted at various points during the day, signaling all was fine on both the home and business front. Jenny did mention Drew and Arianna's money worries had somehow been worked out.

Getting ready for bed, I spread moisturizer on my face as Rob brushed his teeth. I said, "I'm a little concerned about Drew suddenly having access to money. Had he hidden it from the Feds, or does it have something to do with his new venture? Where did it come from?"

"Not something you need to worry about. Knowing him, someplace extremely shady." Rob put his toothbrush in a glass and then kissed the top of my head.

"But Jenny's there."

"He's not going to hurt her. Much as I hate to say anything good about him, he loves his daughter." He leaned against the counter.

"Don't forget the car fiasco."

"When he left the country and gave her his Lamborghini?" Rob laughed. "That was some car."

"Which was then seized by the Feds. And she's been bugging me for her own car for months. As much as I love my daughter, I'm sure she's bending Drew's ear on that same subject. I'm worried about what I might come home to." I hung the towel on the rack and walked back into the bedroom.

"Whatever happens can be undone. No need to worry about it now."

"Easy for you to say. Are you tired?"

"Not especially. Why?"

"Let's sit on the balcony." I put a sweatshirt on over my nightie and walked toward the door.

"Fine by me." Rob yanked the door open, and we stepped onto the sea-sprayed teak deck and settled into the chairs. Rob scooched his closer, and I snuggled against his shoulder.

"Everything seems so weird," I murmured

"Jenny and Drew?"

"The Calhouns. The ship's authorities think nothing happened, yet I can't help but feel something is amiss. Did Butch just have a heart attack? And Dawn ate something bad? Is it as simple as that, and we're suspecting everyone?"

Rob rubbed his hand up and down my arm. "I think maybe we see things that might not be there just because of the last year. Too many bad things happening. Let's focus on us and enjoying our time together."

Chapter 8

We made our way to the metal gangway for our tour in Bonaire. "I can't wait to swim with the fishes."

Rob chuckled. "I don't think that's a good phrase to use."

"What can I say? The presenter showing the underwater videos put me in the mood." I smiled.

"Not quite what I was talking about."

We climbed into a small bus with two other couples, and it whisked us away to the north side of Kralendijk. The guide reminded us of the importance of not touching the coral and told us the place we would be snorkeling was called One Thousand Steps. I gasped, and he laughed. "Don't worry. More like seventy."

I whispered to Rob. "Seventy doesn't sound like a walk in the park either."

"We've been in training on the ship. Piece of cake."

"Which reminds me, I shouldn't have had that ten-layer cake for dessert last night." I groaned.

"We split it. And we'll work it off this morning. One good thing. We're alone." He grinned.

I jerked my head toward the other passengers, and he said, "You know what I mean."

I slid my hand into his and kissed his shoulder.

The guide continued with his spiel as the sparsely decorated scenery interspersed with breathtaking cerulean sea views paraded by the window. We came to a narrow stretch of road with a few parked cars clinging to a slender piece of shoulder on the right and a limestone-walled staircase on the left. The van pulled over as far as possible, and the guide said, "We'll get out here, and the van will pick us up—as you can see, parking is at a premium."

We scooted out with the other passengers, and he handed out snorkel gear. "Wait for a moment. I'll go first. Watch yourselves going down."

The stone, rough-hewn steps hugged the cliffside and were fairly steep, though wider at the beginning than I thought they'd be. With the gear and for safety's sake, we descended single file till we reached the white sand beach below. The guide explained how to don the equipment for anyone unfamiliar with snorkeling. We put on masks and fins and tuned out the world above the sea.

The water teamed with fish and red, green, and blue coral. A camo-colored lizard fish sat on one of the reefs, seemingly as enthralled by us as we were by the sea life. A turtle swam past Rob, playing hide-and-seek with the fan coral and sponges. Then, a school of yellow tail snapper zig-zagged right then left over a parrot fish that gaped as if in surprise.

Two scuba divers were about a hundred yards off and much deeper. I pointed to them, took out my snorkel, and said to Rob, "We need to learn how to do that."

He nodded and put his face back into the water. After about forty-five minutes, I began to feel chilled, so I prodded Rob and pointed toward the beach. We swam in, removed our fins, and exited. "That was wonderful."

The tour guide, who was sitting on an old army blanket on the beach, handed us towels. I first dried my hair, then plopped next to him. "Don't you go in?"

"When I'm with my kids, or if someone is a beginner or needs a buddy, sure. But your group seemed to know what they were doing. See those people out there? Newbies on a private tour—my friend,

Benjamin, is their guide. With that much splashing, they won't see many fish."

Rob and I turned toward where he was pointing. I said, "Is that— no, can't be."

The couple were swimming back to shore, and she was coughing. She lifted her mask and ripped the snorkel from her face. It was Dawn in a very skimpy bikini that showed off her trim build. The man with her laughed as he removed his mask. "You didn't need to swallow the whole ocean."

"Michael." Rob turned toward me. "Maybe the rumors are true."

Their guide ran ahead of them and retrieved towels. Dawn dried her hair and then saw us. "Merry, Rob. What a surprise. Did you enjoy it?"

I nodded as she walked toward us. She explained, "Michael convinced me we were spending too much time inside, and he was right. I'm not the best snorkeler, but this was incredible. So much sea life." She smiled. "Good to be enjoying life again. Our tour continues, so I'll see you later."

She took photos and then walked back to where the guide and Michael were standing. The guide beckoned to a small boat offshore, and it moved closer. They swam out and boarded.

"Now, that was a good idea," Rob said.

I turned toward him.

"Taking pictures of the stairs instead of having to climb them."

I groaned.

Soon, the rest of the snorkelers rejoined us, and we traversed the stairs. As I crested the hill, Rob said, "See. That wasn't so bad."

I held up my hand, trying to catch my breath. "A few years from now... I won't be able to... do that."

"Sure you will." Rob grinned.

The minibus arrived, and we boarded quickly.

"Can't wait to take a shower. The saltwater and sand did a number on me." I scratched my itchy scalp. "Love the shampoo and conditioner on the ship. I'm going to see if I can buy it at home." I tilted my head. "Maybe online, if not in the shops."

"I know what Sheila told you, but Dawn and Michael didn't seem like they were 'together.'" Rob gave a quote mark gesture at the end. "More like friends."

"Huh?" I rested my head on his shoulder.

"No touching. Holding hands. Smoldering glances. You know."

I laughed. "You sound like a romance novel."

"There should be more if people have been engaging in hanky-panky. I rest my case." Rob put his arm around me.

"But what if they don't want anyone to know they are involved?"

"There's that." Rob was pensive.

* * *

White foam kissed the tops of the waves as the ship motored from Bonaire. We relaxed on our balcony, having moved our chairs out of the sun so they hugged the glass door to the room. "Do you think I should call Jenny?" I gazed at the sea, feet resting on Rob's lap.

He massaged them. "If you want to hear her voice, why not? If you want to find out what Drew's up to, no."

"No?"

"You'll put her in the middle, and you and I will spend endless amounts of time discussing it, and we only have five days left on our honeymoon. I can think of many other things I'd rather be doing."

"You've only been a parent for a week, and you're already doing a good job." I leaned forward to kiss his nose. "Trivia again today?"

Rob shrugged. "Sure."

I put my hand in his, and we strolled up the stairs to the lounge. The team who won the other day was already firmly ensconced in the chairs

I'm sure they considered "theirs." Our luck was bad because their team already had the maximum number of players.

Sam and Becky walked in behind us. "Want to play together again?"

"Why not?" Rob said.

We gathered our supplies and sat where we had before. Becky chuckled. "Maybe we should change seats. Our luck wasn't too good."

"We did okay. Today's our day." Sam wrote the team name on the top of the page.

Rob leaned forward. "I'm ready."

The social hostess ran through the rules and gave us the first question. Sam and Rob battled it out in terms of an answer. Becky whispered to me, "Have you seen Dawn and Michael?" She whistled. "Quite the item."

"Huh?"

She extended her index finger toward a grouping of chairs. Dawn and Michael's heads were bent close, deep in conversation. Then, Dawn shook a sheaf of papers in his face, threw them on the table, and stalked from the room. He took his time gathering them and, once done, sat back and stared out the windows. A waiter brought him a beer, which he nursed.

"Maybe there's a snag in their well-crafted plans." Becky's eyebrow rose.

"I'm not sure what you mean." I brushed an errant strand of hair behind my ear.

Becky clicked her tongue. "They must have planned this. Dad dying, her taking over—them becoming so cozy. I don't believe in coincidence, do you?"

"Um—not really."

The social hostess was reading one of the last clues.

Rob said, "Merry, a little help here. Why shouldn't you eat apple cores?"

69

"Cyanide. In the seeds," I said automatically, mind on Michael and Dawn.

"Why would you know that?" Sam wrote the answer on the pad.

I coughed. "Poisoning in town. Not apples, but did some research."

"Tough town," Becky said.

"Usually, it's quite nice. And friendly."

The last question was on sports, so I tuned out the banter between Rob and Sam. They finally agreed on the answer, and we exchanged completed sheets with the team next to us.

"We won!" Sam and Rob exchanged high-fives.

"What about us?" Becky said.

"You and Merry were busy talking, but if you are very nice, we may include you in our largess." Sam laughed.

"Don't you think Michael's lonely? Let's join him." A sly smile slithered across Becky's lips. "Can't have the family attorney sad now, can we?"

"Why would you care?" Sam stood.

"You missed it. Trouble in paradise, and I want to find out what's going on." Becky took her hand and led her toward Michael.

"Are we going with them?" Rob asked.

"What the heck." I followed them.

As we sat, Becky said, "I couldn't help but notice you over here all by yourself, so we decided to fix that."

Sam beckoned the waiter, and we ordered drinks.

"You're always welcome, but there's no need. I was enjoying the view." Michael extended his arm toward the windows.

Becky moved closer to him. "We were playing trivia, and I couldn't help but notice Dawn seemed upset. What happened?"

"I haven't had a chance to congratulate you and Sam on your engagement." He dropped the papers from the table into his briefcase and stood. "I wish you every happiness."

Sam said, "Thanks. We appreciate it."

"Aren't you going to answer my question?" Becky asked.

"Just a difference of opinion on a staff reorganization. Nothing you need to worry about. I have a few things I need to attend to, so I'll see you later." He walked toward the elevators.

"A reorg." Becky put her arm around Sam. "Wonder how that's going to impact Randy."

The waiter put our drinks on the low-slung coffee table. Rob lifted the beer to his lips as Becky stood and said, "We're going to take ours to go. I need to see Randy." She and Sam left the lounge.

"That's not going to be good." I leaned against Rob, and he put his arm around me. I took a sip of wine. "You know what I'd rather have?"

He shook his head.

"Something sweet. We missed lunch, and I'm feeling a bit peckish."

"Can't have that." He stood and extended his hand. "Word on the street is there is cheesecake to be had."

We wandered to the lounge on seven and stopped at the entrance. Cocktail tables by night had been transformed with white linens, pretty teacups, and silver. A pianist played softly, and an extensive buffet dominated the back wall adorned with tiered trays containing finger sandwiches, scones, and several different types of cheesecake. All the tables were taken, but across the room, Sheila beckoned. She was sitting with Michael at a table for four.

Rob whispered, "How hungry are you?"

"Starved." I walked in their direction and sat at the table.

A white-clad waiter handed us a tea menu, and we made our selections.

"This is our first tea. I had no idea how crowded it would be." I put my napkin on my lap.

"Lots of Brits on the boat," Sheila said. "And it's serve yourself from the buffet, so you may as well go up. We've already eaten."

Rob and I perused the laden table. The diminutive sandwich triangles were cucumber, shrimp, or roast beef and cheese. Rob levered several onto his plate, and I took two. The scones were beautiful, but I wanted to try the cheesecake. They had strawberry topped, pumpkin with a cinnamon glaze, and one with blueberry. I took pumpkin, and Rob opted for strawberry. As I turned to return to the table, I spied Sheila's bare foot rubbing against Michael's leg and gasped.

Rob said, "What?"

"Later." I shook my head, and we sat.

"Ooh. Those are tempting," Sheila said. "I stuck to the cucumber sandwiches. But maybe... No. I shouldn't."

I couldn't resist the pumpkin cheesecake, so I tried that first and closed my eyes. "So good." I cut another little bit with my fork and gave it to Rob. "You have to try this."

Michael leaned forward. "Is that the pumpkin? I loved it. A little tang from the cream cheese and then that sweet from the glaze. Heaven."

"It is good," Rob said as he smacked his lips.

"I love you, but that's all I'm going to share. If you want more, you'll have to get your own." I moved my plate an inch or two away from him.

He laughed. "Don't you want to try the strawberry?"

"Don't tempt me." I gazed at Michael. "What is it like having to work on a cruise? Rob and I have been keeping up with what's happening on the home front, but it's not the same."

"It's not a vacation, that's for sure. And Butch's death made it even crazier, but you definitely get perks." He pointed toward the buffet. "Can't beat the food. And the setting. Plus, I get a little downtime. Wasn't the snorkeling great today?"

Sheila stabbed part of a cucumber sandwich with her fork. "Glad you enjoyed yourself. While you were out gallivanting with Dawn, I was stuck here."

"Why? What happened?" I asked.

"Randy needed help with something he was working on. That man and technology." She shook her head. "Barely knows where the 'on' button is. He's lucky he's married to me."

She stood. "I've changed my mind. I'm going to have a piece of that cheesecake." She went to the buffet.

Michael frowned as he watched her go. Then he stood and followed her. "I think I'll get something else too."

"That was interesting," I said to Rob.

He whispered, "I think I'm missing something."

"When we get back to the room." I took a last sip of tea. "And maybe this would be a good time to leave."

Sheila put her now full plate down, and I rose. "Thanks for inviting us to share your table. The tea was wonderful."

Rob waved to Michael on our way out.

I said, "That family is just plain weird."

"What happened?"

"Everyone's talking about Dawn and Michael, but I think something is going on between Michael and Sheila." I told him about the way Sheila had rubbed Michael's leg with her foot.

Chapter 9

Rob and I decided on a late dinner since we had tea mid-afternoon. The people who had come early were just leaving, which meant we could score a table by the window. Even though it was dark outside, occasional flashes of white decorated the waves.

The waiter held my chair as I sat and admired the chargers. They were something that would have been at home in Neptune's castle under the sea. Dreamy blues and golds swirled against a cream background. I wrestled with the overly large menu and said, "This is going to take me a while. I want everything."

Rob nodded, engrossed in selecting his choices. "I think I'll start with escargot, have a Caesar salad, and then the roasted pork tenderloin."

The waiter approached. I asked, "Can you have the seafood risotto as an appetizer portion?"

"Of course, madam."

"I'll have that, the Caesar salad, and the herb-crusted lamb."

He put a bread basket on the table and poured wine.

I said, "Good. They have two of the salted rolls. I'd hate to fight you for one, dearest husband of mine."

"I fear it would be a fight to the death because those are that good." He broke off a piece and buttered it. "What's the plan for tomorrow?"

"Dominica. We'll go river tubing and then see a waterfall."

"Sounds like fun."

"Oh no." I turned toward the window.

"What?"

"Randy and Sheila coming this way."

Sheila said, "Fancy meeting you two. Guess everyone's eating late after tea this afternoon."

"It was filling." I smiled as I waited for them and the Maître D' to move away.

Sheila motioned to the table behind Rob. "Can we sit here by the window?"

The Maître D' said, "Of course, madam." He pulled out the chair for her.

Rob whispered, "At least they're not sitting with us."

"And there's enough room between tables—we should be able to converse normally." I nodded. "But they're still a little too close for comfort."

Our hors d'oeuvres arrived, and we dug in. "This risotto is terrific." I spooned some onto Rob's bread plate. "You have to try it."

"I told you we just happened to meet at tea. There wasn't anything to it." Sheila's voice carried as she was facing me.

Randy mumbled something, and Sheila said, "He's just a friend. He works for you. I'm not stupid."

"He works for Dawn. I don't want you getting too close to him." Randy's voice rose.

"Isn't it better to have someone trying to figure out what they're doing? I don't know about you, but if Dawn's already talking about a reorg, someone might find himself out on the streets. Or without the team he has now." Sheila jabbed a finger into Randy's chest.

He kissed it. "I'm sorry. I trust you. It's just my head's spinning. All this change."

Sheila grinned like a cat whose owner had forgotten to put away the cream. "I'm always thinking of you, baby. You know that."

He murmured something.

"But you need to rely on me. Slipping Dawn aloin was stupid. What if someone had found out?" Her voice dropped, and I couldn't make out what else she said.

He had poisoned Dawn. I knew it. Had they done something to Butch?

Rob waved his hand in front of my face. "Earth to Merry. What's going on?"

"Didn't you hear that?" I whispered.

"Some." He shrugged.

"I'll tell you later."

The rest of the dinner was delicious yet uneventful, and when we exited, Randy and Sheila were cooing like a couple of lovebirds. As soon as we left the restaurant, I turned to Rob. "Did you hear her tell Randy he shouldn't have used the aloin on Dawn?"

He shook his head and his eyes widened. "I missed that part."

"And they're worried about what the reorg will mean for him. What if he tries something else? What if he killed his father? We have to tell Dawn."

"I agree, but from what we just saw, those two have nothing on their minds but going to bed. We'll talk to her tomorrow."

"You're right." I glanced at my phone. "Show's already started; want to slip in late?"

He nodded, and we traversed the ship to the theater, stopping a few times to peer into the glitzy shop windows showing the latest in cruise wear and sparkly baubles. The casino was doing a brisk business and, as we arrived at the theater, we slid into seats in the back.

The comedian was in the middle of his act, talking about the absurdity of the ship's laundromat. The crowd guffawed, seeming to agree with him. I murmured, "Going to have to check that out."

"You want to do laundry?"

"It sounds like an adventure." I smiled.

The comedian continued, and I let my eyes wander around the crowd. Becky and Sam were laughing a few rows ahead of us, and Michael and Dawn were a few rows ahead of them, seemingly in deep conversation. I pointed. "I don't think everyone's enjoying the show."

The person next to Rob said, "Shhh."

"Sorry." I pantomimed, zipping my lips.

* * *

I completed my morning stretches on the floor next to the bed, gazing at the bustling port outside our balcony door. Thatched hut kiosks were set up along the pier and on the street leading to the dock, with brightly colored t-shirts fluttering in the breeze. Merchants were ready to sell their wares to souvenir-hunting tourists.

"It must be strange." I frowned

Rob was reading the day's newsletter on top of the bed. "What?"

"To know Butch's body is still on board."

"That's what happens when you go to the smaller islands. They likely don't have the facilities to take the body. Or it could be Dawn's asked them to keep him on board till we get back. It's only four more days till we return to Miami, and his body's been refrigerated. It'll be easier to ship him back from there."

"I would think they'd want closure. Kind of tough to move on when he's still downstairs. They must feel like they're in a bit of a holding pattern." I stood. "We should get going. The tour will be leaving soon."

Rob pointed to his swim trunks. "All I have to do is put on my water shoes."

I moved to the walk-in closet and put on my bathing suit and cover-up. "I think this cruise line is going to spoil me for any other."

"You may need to lower your expectations because we don't have the kind of money Mac and my mom do."

I sat on his lap and put my arms around his neck. "We have each other. And Jenny. And that's worth a lot more than all this." I laughed. "Maybe."

He kissed me and said, "If you don't get up, we're going to miss the tour."

"Heaven forbid." I slid my feet into water shoes and stood. "Ready."

We walked to the theater and waited for our tour number to be called. Randy, Sheila, Becky, and Sam stood by the stage. I whispered, "Is it wrong to hope they won't be with us?"

"Not at all," Rob replied.

They called our number, and we followed the woman holding the corresponding sign to the buses stationed at the end of the pier. I rolled my eyes. "We're going to be one happy family, with just two missing."

Someone called, "Wait up."

I turned. It was Dawn and Michael. We slowed our pace, and I groaned, "How fun. Together again." Dawn was vibrant in a pink suit with a fuchsia and lime sheer cover-up, and Michael wore a t-shirt and lime green board shorts.

Rob said, "No lacking for style on this tour."

Dawn gave him an uncertain smile. "I guess I should be wearing more black, but who takes that on a cruise to the Caribbean?"

The bus dropped us off near a rocky shore where small inner tubes abounded. We were near the last to leave, so we watched as workers handed tour participants faded red life jackets and helmets of different hues. Then they situated each person on top of blue and yellow one-person tubes complete with handles and a small wooden oar.

"Patrick took the girls rafting the Salt River when we were in Phoenix, and Jenny enjoyed it. I've never done it before, have you?" I stepped forward in line.

"Once before, on the Umpqua River in Oregon. It was a class four rapid, with something called a pinball. Exciting." Rob smiled.

"Scale of ten?"

"Six, not including Class A, which is basically lake water."

I cast a worried glance at the placid river in front of us. "This isn't going to be like that, is it?"

"Walk in the park—when I rafted in Oregon, there were six of us to a raft plus a guide. Nothing like this. Not to worry."

One man pushed the inflatable and its rider into the current as other aides in bright yellow were spaced strategically along the river to help anyone who ran aground or tipped over. From our vantage point, it was a colorful game of bumper pool with live participants. Then it was our turn. We walked into the water, being careful of our footing due to the rocky coast. I hopped onto my raft, using the handholds, and situated myself dead center on the tube. Rob followed on his, and then we floated down the calm river.

He held onto my foot as we meandered together. "This isn't as bad as I thought."

I smiled.

We neared what must have been a problem area, and one of the helpers pushed us back into the more swiftly moving water. The pace picked up, and Rob and I were disconnected as the sound of rushing water increased and began to roar. Our tubes bobbed like corks, and we were tossed left and right. My heart pounded, and I tried to use the oar they had given to steer but eventually gave up as it didn't seem to matter what I did, the river was going to take me where it wanted.

My raft banged into Rob's as we came out of a particularly rough spot. He was grinning from ear to ear. "That was great!"

"It got the adrenaline going. That's for sure." The guides pushed us toward the shore to regroup before the next set of rapids.

Sam shouted to Rob, "How'd you like it?"

Rob gave her a thumbs up.

Becky was a drowned rat, but she laughed. "Hit a wall of water somewhere in there."

Dawn seemed stunned, and Michael made his way toward her by pushing off other rafts.

Sheila and Randy had planted their feet firmly on each other's raft, effectively joining them together. After the rest of the riders caught up, guides began to push us back into the river. Dawn was one of the first to go, Michael was a few people behind her, Randy and Sheila spun merrily into the current, and Sam and Becky followed.

Rob and I were a few past them. Again, it was smooth sailing for a short stretch, and I enjoyed watching the lush landscape roll by. Evergreens and palms were intermixed with long grasses, and purple-throated hummingbirds cavorted near iguanas sunning themselves on rocks lining the shoreline.

"I could get used to this," I said as Rob and I intertwined hands.

"It is peaceful," he replied.

The sound of water rose again, and I dropped his hand, determined to get the paddle to do work. Before long, we were rushing downstream, and all of a sudden, we spied a riderless raft off to the left, caught in the shoals. Rob maneuvered himself toward shore, grabbed my raft, and pulled it and me out of the current.

"Who does the raft belong to?" Rob stood, hanging onto his inner tube. He scanned the boulders and rocks near us. I wiggled myself off my raft and joined him. I spied something pink that would have been hidden from people whizzing by—it was wedged between two boulders on the right. I pointed.

Rob said, "Take my hand and see if you can reach whoever that is."

A man careened past and shouted, "Trouble?"

Rob nodded.

"I'll tell the guides to come back."

Rob and I formed a short human chain. I leaned out as far as possible and struck what I thought was a leg. I groped, grabbed fabric, and pulled. The person floated free and moved toward me, face up in a life jacket. Rob yanked me toward him and then grabbed the person I had found. It was Dawn, and she had a gash on her forehead.

She coughed and opened her eyes. "Where am I?"

Rob said, "Something must have happened. You were on a tube in the river. Do you remember?"

She nodded and then grabbed her forehead. "A rock."

"You hit a rock?" I asked.

"Maybe. Or a rock hit me."

Rob helped her to her feet. "The guides should be back any minute. They can take you to the hospital to get checked out."

"The ship's doctor can do that. I'd rather go there."

Three guides ran toward us on the shore. "Are you okay, Miss?"

"Just a bit banged up."

Rob helped her to the bank.

"There's a road not far. Can you make it? Then we'll take you for help."

"Just take me back to the ship."

"Dawn, I'll come with you." I started to climb onto the shore.

"Nonsense. I'm fine. You and Rob go on."

She had regained color, so I turned to Rob. He said, "Up to you."

"Really. I'll be okay, and you can check on me later. Promise." Dawn turned and walked away between the two guides.

The third slid into the water. "If you climb back onto your rafts, I'll push you into the current."

We complied and were soon rushing downstream. When we arrived at the next way station, Michael was standing in the water, scanning the area behind us. He asked, "Have you seen Dawn? I lost track of her, and she hasn't come by. I could have sworn she was in front of me. You were behind us, weren't you?"

"She's okay. She had a bump on her forehead, and two of the guides took her back to the ship."

He hopped off his raft, waded to one of the other guides, and they had a terse conversation. Michael climbed onto the bank and turned to us. "He's going to have one of his friends come get me and take me to the ship. Can you bring Dawn's and my things back with you from the bus?"

We nodded.

Sheila, Randy, Sam, and Becky were further away, toward the front of the group, and chatting amongst themselves. Sheila glanced over her shoulder at one point but didn't ask any questions. And then the guides pushed us into the river again.

Rob and I meandered along, waiting for the next set of rapids. I asked, "Don't you think they would have wondered where Dawn was?"

"Probably didn't even notice she was gone."

"But they must have seen Michael leave."

Rob shrugged, and then we were back into the rapids. I spun around like a top, and then one of the guides pushed me toward the center. Water splashed my face, and it felt like I was riding against a wave machine. Finally, the river became calm, and the guides pushed our rafts toward shore and the waiting buses. I handed my raft to one of the guides and wandered toward a stack of towels. I grabbed one and dried my hair and face, laughing. "Got soaked on that last."

"Not the only one." Rob was dripping and took the towel from me as the guides handed out rum punches and sodas. We sat on a bench to enjoy ours and dry off.

Sheila walked toward us. "What happened to Dawn and Michael?"

I told her.

"It was rough in a couple of places. That's too bad. Do you think we should try to go back to the ship or continue?" she asked.

"Your call. Dawn seemed okay when she left, and Michael did go after her." Rob shrugged.

"We'll stay then. I'll let the others know." She walked away.

"Why on earth did she ask us if they should stay?" I asked Rob.

"Strange people." He finished his drink and extended his hand for my empty. We stood and headed to the bus, dropping our trash in the garbage as we went.

I climbed aboard, retrieved the bags Michael and Dawn had left, put them with ours so we'd remember, and sat. The rest of our group made their way to their seats, and the bus took off, tour guide giving a good overview of the island on the way to the falls. Misty clouds seemed to caress the tops of the mountains as we drove further inland.

The bus stopped at the falls, and people queued for the restrooms. Afterward, I rejoined Rob by a little shack, and then we walked to where the group was waiting near an overlook guarded by a rusty handrail.

A beautiful white stream rushed in and out of boulders and launched itself from the cliff to the pristine waiting pool at the bottom. Primordial green ferns, moss, and aubergine elephant ears formed a perfect backdrop.

The tour guide directed us to a set of steep stone stairs with wooden posts. I laughed and turned back to Rob. "Oh, good. More stairs." We followed the group to the landing area below and navigated slippery stones to the base of the waterfall. The temperature cooled a good ten degrees between the shade and the mist blowing off the water.

Randy sidled up to Rob. "What do you think happened to Dawn?"

"Don't know. Said she hit her head, not sure how it happened."

"Did you see anything when you were coming down?"

"Just her raft. That's what made us stop. Then we found her."

"Did she say anything else?" Randy persisted.

"Said it was a rock like Merry told Sheila." As people began to climb the steps to leave, Rob moved closer to the waterfall for a better shot.

"She hit a rock? Did she tip or something?" Randy moved in front of Rob, ruining his picture.

"Randy, I don't know. You can ask her when you get back to the ship. Now move, if you don't mind, I'd like to get a good photo."

Randy brushed past me on his way to the stairs.

Rob finished and walked toward me. "I didn't think that guy was going to give up. What else could I have told him?"

* * *

Rob stopped to get coffee, and I returned to the room to shower and change. As I walked past the desk in our suite, I tripped over a sneaker I must not have pushed all the way under. I fell, and the bags I had been carrying flew from my hands.

"Crap." I rubbed the elbow I landed on and sat cross-legged on the floor, surveying the papers, t-shirts, and mementos we had bought, which were now strewn haphazardly around me. *What were those papers? We hadn't brought reading material on the tour.* Michael and Dawn's bags were nearby—maybe they were theirs? I crawled toward them, stuffing our things back into shopping bags as I went.

It was a draft of a memo from Dawn to the people at Butch's company. I skimmed it. She wrote about how saddened she was by his death and how disappointed she was Randy had decided to leave the firm. *What? Randy hadn't mentioned leaving. Was she forcing him out?*

The door to the room opened, and Rob said, "I thought you might want to try an affogato. It has ice cream... What are you doing on the floor? Are you okay?"

He put the coffees on the desk and held out his hand. "Need help getting up?"

"Thanks." I stood. "I tripped over my shoe. But I found this." I handed him the piece of paper.

Rob read the memo. "Where did you get it?"

"It was in either Michael or Dawn's bag. When I tripped, it must have come out. What do you think it means? Randy hasn't acted like he was leaving the firm. Do you think he changed his mind?"

"Either that or Dawn's buying him out."

"Which bag do I put it back in? I don't want them to think I was going through their stuff."

Someone knocked, and Rob opened the door. It was the butler for Dawn's suite. He said, "Ms. Franklin sent me to retrieve their things—she didn't want to trouble you."

I gestured to the still-messy floor. "I took a tumble and, although I know what's ours, I'm not sure what belongs to which bag."

"If you collect your things, I'll bring the rest back, and they can sort it out."

I picked up our few remaining items, and then he took the rest and left. I sank onto the bed. "Well, I guess they're going to know we saw the memo now."

"All they'll know is their stuff ended up on the floor." Rob pointed toward the bed. "What's that—a present?"

There was a sturdy gray box on the bed with a peek-a-boo window with tissue paper blocking the view.

"Did you get me something?" I smiled at Rob.

"Not recently." He lifted the lid. The laundry we had left in the bag on our bed was freshly washed and pressed, each piece delicately wrapped with tissue paper. He shrugged, "No present—just clothes we already had."

I lifted one of my shirts. "Almost as good as a present—someone else washed and folded them."

Rob stared at me like I was nuts. "Let's shower and change. Then we'll stop by Dawn's suite to check on her."

✳ ✳ ✳

Dawn opened the door. "Every time you come to the suite, you check to see how I am. I feel like an awful nuisance for such a young person. But I'm going to change that. I'd like you to attend a small cocktail party

85

and dinner tonight. We'll start here, and then dinner will be served in a private dining room. Please say you'll come."

On the one hand, I wanted to be alone with Rob. On the other, it was always fun to see how the other half lived. Plus, I was concerned about Dawn. I glanced at Rob, and he raised his right eyebrow. "We'll come," I said.

She walked away from the door, and we followed to the living room. "Something to drink? The butler makes a refreshing cucumber seltzer."

"I'll try that," I said as I sat on the couch.

"Make it two," Rob echoed and joined me.

She sat on the chair opposite us and tapped into her phone. "Won't take long."

"You appear to be better than you were earlier." Rob motioned to her forehead.

"Oh, this." Her hand fluttered to her face. "Just a scratch. I feel fine."

I leaned toward her. "But you blacked out."

"Just for a moment. No headache, so it can't be too bad." She crossed her legs. "Thanks for bringing our bags back. I hope it wasn't too much trouble."

"I guess you heard I dropped them."

"The butler mentioned it. No worries, we got everything sorted."

As if he'd heard us talking of him, the door opened, and the butler walked in carrying three tall drinks, each garnished with a slice of cucumber on the rim. He bowed, putting the tray at eye level, and each of us took a glass. Then he withdrew.

I sipped. It was like cucumber water but fizzier. And he had muddled mint at the bottom. "Delicious."

"I'm glad you like it." Dawn smiled.

Rob cleared his throat. "Have you remembered anything more about this morning?"

"Not really." She shook her head. "I went through a particularly rough patch where it felt like I was going to lose the tube, but I held on, and then boom. I hit something. Or something hit me, and I was out. I woke, staring at Merry." She frowned. "I didn't ask. What were you doing there?"

"Rob saw the empty raft and maneuvered us toward the shore. Then we pulled you in."

"Thank you for stopping. I'm not sure what would have happened if you hadn't found me."

"I'm glad you ended face up in the life jacket." I shivered. "And I'm not sure how to tell you this, so I'm just going to say it. The last time we were here, we warned you about Randy, but we weren't sure. Now I am. He did put aloin in the food you ate in his suite. He told Sheila about it last night, and I overheard them."

"He put something in my food? Why would he do that? We were friends."

"He'd learned you were taking over. Maybe he was upset." Rob shrugged.

She stood and paced. "Was he trying to kill me?" Her face paled. "Did he kill his father?" She sank back onto the chair. "Did he have anything to do with what happened this morning? It's all a fog."

"We don't know the answers to your questions, but we wanted you to know so you can protect yourself. You shouldn't trust him."

"Michael's been trying to get me to buy him out. He had a bad feeling about him. I've been resisting because Butch wouldn't have wanted me to. He would have wanted Randy to remain with the firm. But this puts a different spin on it. If he was willing to poison me..."

I glanced at my watch. "We had wanted to see the lecture this afternoon, but if you want us to stay, we will."

"No, no. I've taken enough of your time as it is. And on your honeymoon," she tsked. "I need time to think about this anyway." She stood and walked us to the door. "Thanks again. And don't forget, cocktails at five-thirty. I'll feel better if you're there, especially since Randy is coming."

Chapter 10

As Rob lifted his hand to ring the doorbell, I asked, "Do I look okay?" I had dithered in front of my abbreviated wardrobe and finally decided on an emerald-green dress Jenny had packed for a special dinner—I figured this was just the occasion. It had a scoop neck that highlighted the necklace Rob had given me the previous Valentine's Day. My red curly locks were held on one side with a rhinestone comb I was afraid was too flashy.

Rob kissed my cheek. "You'll be the most beautiful woman in the room. Like always."

He pressed the button, and the butler answered. "Mr. Jenson and Ms. March. The guests are in the living room."

We walked into the room, and I was glad I had taken extra time on my appearance. Everyone was dressed to the nines. A tuxedo-clad man played the piano, and glasses clinked as the ice was added. Dawn walked toward us, arm extended, wearing a striking form-fitting long black and white dress with a slit up the side. "Merry, Rob, so glad you came." She was a little pale and had a small bandage over the gash on her forehead but otherwise seemed okay. She gave us a quick hug. "I think you know everyone."

Rob nodded, and I smiled. Randy lifted his glass to us.

He was so brazen. How could he stand here in Dawn's suite knowing he poisoned her? And how could she act as if nothing had happened? The rich are just plain weird. I took the glass of champagne the butler offered and shuffled even closer to Rob.

Sam and Becky were on the couch, holding hands, and Michael stood next to the door to the balcony, ignoring us and staring at the sea. The large dining room table had been transformed into a buffet, and soft black and turquoise cloths had been artfully draped to evoke an ocean scene. The centerpiece was a seahorse ice carving. Rob walked closer to the sculpture. "This is detailed."

"They carved it this afternoon. It is special, isn't it?" Dawn extended her hand. "Please, help yourselves—there's enough food here to feed an army."

Sheila loaded caviar onto a mother-of-pearl spoon from the varied spread. There were heaping platters of shrimp, raw oysters on the half-shell, and crab legs. Another section held an assortment of cheese and crackers, and further down was fruit and charcuterie shaped into roses.

"Makes me feel bad to spoil something so carefully crafted, but I'm going to." I lifted a small plate and took shrimp, gouda, and a few water crackers. Rob followed and opted for the raw oysters, melon, and prosciutto. We sat next to Becky and Sam on the couch.

Sheila perched on the chair next to us. "I can't believe you didn't take the caviar. It's terrific, and one of those," she pointed to the shrimp," is double the calories of what's on my little spoon."

"But it's your fifth 'little' bite and, besides, Merry's got a great little figure—she doesn't need to worry about her weight." Randy sat on the arm of Sheila's chair and dug into the salumi and roast beef on his plate.

I worried it would break under his girth, but he didn't seem concerned. Dawn gathered a few grapes from the buffet and sat in the chair opposite Sheila and Randy. Michael walked away from the window and pulled one of the dining room chairs next to Dawn.

Sam said, "Heard you took a spill this morning on the tubing adventure. How are you feeling?"

"Fine. Just a gash." Dawn touched the gauze on her forehead. "What did you two do this afternoon?"

"Lazed by the pool. We searched for Rob and Merry to play trivia, but I guess they were getting ready for this shindig."

I shrugged. "Guilty. What do you and Becky think of the art on the ship?"

"The art in the common areas, and come to think of it, this suite, is beautiful." Sam stood and walked to a large piece hanging over the piano. "Love the brush strokes and color. So vibrant."

"But if you're talking about the stuff they sell on board, not so much." Becky wandered to the buffet, selecting caviar and a toast point before returning to her seat. "It's okay, but it's designed for the masses. Not something you'd want. They work on the excitement, hype, and thrill of auctions to create a kind of bidding hysteria. Works for them—not so much for you."

"Didn't you buy something today, Sheila?" Randy elbowed her.

She turned beet red. "Uh, the guy said it was a rare piece. Lots of people bid—"

"Oh, I didn't mean..." Becky stuttered.

"It's okay." Sheila frowned. "I guess I have plebian taste."

"I'm sure it's beautiful." Becky continued.

Sam changed the subject. "Who wants to see the magician tonight? I heard he's terrific."

"I had the butler reserve seats for us in the front row," Dawn said.

"How thoughtful." Rob squeezed my hand.

"I just thought it would be nice. If anyone doesn't want to go, it's fine."

Michael squeezed Dawn's bare shoulder. "I think it will be great."

"Suck up," Sheila said under her breath, yet audible enough for me to hear.

I started and then said, "We appreciate it. I think the show will be wonderful."

The butler announced, "You may want to adjourn to the study, where dinner will be served."

We took the elevator to the private dining room, which was adjacent to the main one. A large table dominated the space, with linens using the same ocean scheme as the buffet in Dawn's suite. Cream-colored bookshelves lined one wall and were filled with carefully curated art objects. On the right, at the far end of the table, was an entire wall of windows that showcased the crashing sea below. A small tufted brown leather couch faced out to take in the drama, and two armchairs completed the tableau.

A waiter handed us glasses of champagne, but Sheila shook her head and said, "Enough with the champagne. Can I get a vodka martini?"

"Of course. Blue cheese olives?"

She nodded, and he gestured to another waiter who had just entered. "Martini for the lady."

Randy said, "Scotch for me. Neat."

He nodded and left for the bar.

I took a glass of champagne and walked to the view. Rob joined me. "Beautiful, isn't it."

"It is. And it would be so peaceful if..." I murmured.

"Let's try to enjoy ourselves in the middle of all these family dynamics. But tomorrow, it's just you and me, kid."

I grinned. "Deal."

"Would everyone please be seated? There are names at the top of the plates," The head waiter instructed.

Rob scanned the seahorses holding discrete white tags and then beckoned to me. "We're down here."

Dawn was at one head of the table, closest to the door. No one was seated at the other end, though a place had been laid. Michael was to her right, and Sheila was next to him, then Randy. On Dawn's left were Becky, Sam, me, and Rob. No one sat opposite Rob.

The waiter returned with Randy and Sheila's drinks, and Dawn stood. "I'd like to propose a toast." She pointed to the empty place at the table's other end. "To Butch, may you rest in peace and enjoy all of heaven's comfort and joy."

We stood as one and raised our glasses. "To Butch."

"Like that bastard's going to heaven," Sheila murmured to Randy.

My mouth dropped. How could she say that about her deceased father-in-law? Randy didn't even flinch. How had he really felt about his father?

Dawn paled, so she had heard the comment. I waited for her to object, to say something in defense of her husband, but she stayed mum, hands below the table.

"Dad is in heaven. I'm sure of it." Becky stated.

Sam put her arm around her. "How sure are you?" She nuzzled her ear. "After what he said about us?"

I bit the inside of my cheek. This was going downhill fast, and Rob and I might end up with deluxe seats by ourselves for the show. Michael sat back in his chair, expressionless as if he were used to this.

Becky batted Sam's arm away. "He was wrong about us. But that was just his age. He's never been very accepting. But otherwise, he was a good dad. After Mom left, he took care of us. He loved us."

Sam's face grew red. "My parents are the same age. And they welcomed us with open arms."

"Plus, you have a different recollection than me." Randy sipped his drink. "Probably because you were younger and a girl. All he did was work. In fact, I can't remember one ball game of mine he came to. All the other dads were there but not him."

"He was making money for us. So, we could live comfortably and have the things we wanted." Becky moved closer to the table.

"I went to work for him. I was never enough. Not one word of praise." Randy rubbed the back of his neck. "I thought it would be different—I brought in new clients. Helped. Still nothing. And now this." He extended his hand toward Dawn.

Her cheeks flared pink, but she pointedly stared at the menu. "Getting late. We should order if we want to attend the show."

The rest of the dinner held fewer fireworks than the earlier portion of the evening, and somehow, we made it through. Rob and I trailed behind the rest of the group as we traversed the ship to the theater. He leaned close to my ear. "We could make a break for it."

"Tempting, but I do want to see this guy. Plus, we'll have front-row seats. How bad could it be?"

We walked into the venue and were ushered to our seats. A waiter asked if we wanted anything. Rob and I ordered Bailey's and the others their libation of choice. The after-dinner drinks arrived, and the show started.

The magician started small, with some card tricks, and then a detailed rope one where the ends kept multiplying. I couldn't see how he did it as much as I concentrated and as close as we were. I turned to Rob. "That's amazing."

"He's going to explain some of the tricks tomorrow afternoon—want to go?"

"Of course. Maybe we can learn and try them out on Jenny."

The magician asked for a volunteer from the audience. Sheila raised Randy's arm, and he glared at her. "What are you doing?"

"That man right there." The magician pointed to Randy.

He groaned, got to his feet, and climbed the stairs to the stage. The magician gestured to a seat opposite him. They both sat.

"Would you say you're susceptible, sir?"

"Not especially."

"Get good sleep last night?"

"Okay."

"Been hypnotized before?"

"Don't believe in that nonsense." Randy started to stand.

"Do it, honey, sit down," Sheila pleaded.

He sat. "Okay. For her."

The magician spoke in a slow melodic manner and had Randy fixate on a space in the distance. Before long, the magician told him, "You're so tired, close your eyes and let your head drop. When I say wake, you'll be refreshed and ready to go."

Randy's head lolled.

"Think back to two nights ago. What happened?"

"I slept." Randy's voice was a monotone.

"Earlier. Around four-thirty. What did you do?"

Randy chuckled. "Dawn coming for drinks."

"What was funny?"

"Put the yellow junk from the aloe plant on the shrimp. Serves her right. Merry called later and told me how sick Dawn got." He snorted. "Good gag."

My mouth dropped. Becky, Sam, and Michael appeared stunned while Dawn studied her hands.

Sheila shouted. "Stop this right now!"

The magician said, "One, two, three, wake."

Randy's eyes opened, and he stretched and smiled as if refreshed.

Dawn stood and strode from the theater, and Michael trailed her, speaking non-stop.

"Let's thank Randy, Ladies and Gentlemen."

There was a smattering of applause as people tried to figure out what had just happened. Randy left the stage, and Sheila met him at the bottom of the stairs. "You idiot!" She grabbed his hand, and they left.

The magician began another trick without missing a beat.

Sam and Becky glanced at Rob and me, and we shrugged. They got up and left.

"What do you want to do?" Rob whispered.

"Might as well stay."

* * *

I unscrewed the cap to my make-up remover, applied it to my eyes, and wiped it off with a tissue. Rob leaned against the counter. "That wasn't something you see every day."

"How do you think she got the magician to do it?"

"Who convinced him? Not sure—Dawn or Michael?"

"Definitely her. He was as shocked as Becky and Sam." I put toothpaste on the toothbrush and then passed the tube to Rob.

"Wonder what the cruise line thought of the show. No one but our group knew what was going on." I started brushing.

"I'm sure they were surprised. It's a good thing the rest of his show was great, otherwise he might have explaining to do."

"Uh-huh. What's Dawn going to do next?" I swished with mouthwash.

"No telling. But one thing's clear."

I lifted my eyebrow.

"Her reorg is not going to include him."

Chapter 11

The waiter draped a white cloth onto the table on the balcony and quickly followed with an entire setup of knives, forks, etc. Then he placed a basket of pastries and a bowl of fresh fruit in the center, which was accented with an orchid bloom. Last came our covered breakfasts. Rob had opted for eggs over easy and crispy bacon; I went for a poached egg and corned beef hash. We shared the sourdough toast and black cherry jam.

"A bit of a come down from last night's extravaganza, but I guess it will do." I smiled as I buttered the toast. "Could have gone to the caviar breakfast—it is Sunday."

Rob shook his head. "Nope. You're mine today. Having breakfast here ensures we won't run into anyone else."

The doorbell rang.

"A little too soon to be collecting our tray." Rob started to stand.

"I'll get it." I tossed my napkin on the chair, walked to the door, and opened it.

"I hope I'm not disturbing you." Dawn was at the door. "You didn't have a 'do not disturb sign' up, and I wanted to explain about yesterday."

"We were having breakfast." I pointed.

She backed away. "Maybe later would be better."

"Come in. Have you eaten?"

"The butler brought me something earlier."

I walked toward the balcony. It seemed like we were destined to be part of this group forever. All Rob and I wanted was time on our own, but Dawn had dark bags under her eyes, and her face was pasty. I couldn't turn her away.

Dawn trailed me, head turning right and left. "Wow. This is small."

"Seemed big to me. Until I saw your spread." Rob pulled the chaise closer to the table. "Sorry, we only have two chairs, and since we're eating...."

"I'll only take a few moments of your time." She paused. "Please continue—I don't want everything to get cold."

I cut into my egg, and it oozed onto the hash.

"You must think I'm awful for last night. I racked my brain for how to let Randy know I knew he was responsible for making me sick. If I told him you overheard, he might have taken it out on you. But I couldn't continue to pretend as if nothing had happened. It felt like I was walking on eggshells around him.

"The magician's write-up said he was also a hypnotist. I had my butler reach out, and he came to my suite yesterday afternoon. He agreed to play along. Needless to say, there was a cost."

"Wasn't the cruise line upset? People were pretty confused; it wasn't the normal chicken clucking." I broke off a piece of toast and dabbed it in the yolk.

"The hotel director stopped by last night. He asked that I refrain from changing the entertainment again. He also asked if I wanted to press charges against Randy. I told him no. Even with what Randy admitted to doing, he said he had to apologize to Randy on behalf of the cruise line." She shrugged. "Slapped my hand. No big deal."

Rob finished his last piece of bacon and turned to face Dawn better. "I don't understand how you knew Randy would volunteer."

"I knew Sheila would make him do it. She always wants them to be front and center. They came with us to Vegas a year ago, and she made Randy raise his hand for a card trick the guy did. Plus, I hedged my bets and told the magician to pick him even if he didn't volunteer." Dawn smiled. "At any rate, it worked."

"What's next?" I asked.

"After we get Butch home and buried, I'll make sure I don't have to see Randy again. Michael's mad I didn't alert him to my plan last night. But I knew he'd try to talk me out of it. He's worried about what Randy might do to me. You heard how he talked about his father last night, so Michael thinks it's not too big of a stretch to assume Randy killed Butch. I can't see it, but I guess he could have." She shuddered. "But the doctor is convinced it wasn't murder. I don't know who to believe."

She stood. "I've taken enough of your time."

Rob followed her to the door and shut it after she left.

I took one last bite of toast and joined him in the room. "What did you think of that?"

"She got a very public confession that Randy tried to harm her. And if she chose, she could make a case for attempted murder. I think she's a very clever woman. If she wanted him to leave the company without having to buy him out, she's got tremendous leverage now."

I sat on the bed to put on my shoes. "Could she have killed Butch?"

"She's the one who benefits most."

✳ ✳ ✳

I eyed the tall tower with trepidation—Rob nudged me as the line through the trees had moved, and I hadn't. I crept forward. It might have been my imagination, but as I grew closer, the tower seemed higher. And the ladder to climb it went straight up. I gulped and lagged the queue again.

"Merry, this is supposed to be fun. If you don't want to do this, we don't have to." Rob rubbed my shoulder.

"But you've been looking forward to it."

"I have, but I love you more." He smiled.

I faced the ladder and began to climb. "Not as bad as I thought," I huffed. After the tenth rung, I began to have my doubts—but I soldiered on.

We reached the top, and I took a moment to recover my breath. "Seriously need...to...cut down on...the carbs."

The Guadeloupean guide motioned me forward and helped me put on the protective equipment. "Are you sure about this?" I tugged on the straps.

Jungle crowded the zipline, which disappeared into the lush foliage, and bird song rang, almost drowning out the fast thumping of my heart.

Rob moved closer and pulled on my harness. "Seems solid to me."

"I mean this." I gestured to the high line I was about to be hooked to.

The attendant said, "Don't forget, you need to ring the bell when you get to the next stopping point, so he'll know it's safe to come."

"Are you sure you want me to go first? Maybe you should." I eyed the distance to the ground nervously.

"If I go last, I'll know if you fell." Rob chuckled, and I glared at him.

He pulled me close. "I repeat, if you don't want to do it, we don't have to. We can climb back down." He gestured to the steep ladder we had already scaled, crowded with people awaiting their turn.

I gritted my teeth and allowed the attendant to strap me to the line. Then, he told me to grab the bar above my head and to jump off the platform. *Jump off the platform? Was he nuts?* I gripped the bar as if my life depended on it and every muscle in my body tensed. People were waiting, so I knew I'd have to leap soon. I jumped, and my heart went into my throat. Leaves whizzed past my face, and the air under the canopy became cooler.

Everything felt sturdy—I wasn't going to fall. I began to relax and enjoy the ride. All too soon, I came upon the next platform, and my line slackened, slowing me down. I climbed aboard and rang the bell. A few moments later, Rob joined me.

"That was great!" I beamed.

Rob chuckled. "Ready for number two?"

"You bet." I cannonballed off the platform, and the line jerked as it became taut. My attention was drawn to a blue and yellow macaw high in the canopy, a black and red woodpecker whose incessant knocking filled the air, and a purple-throated hummingbird, feasting on a delicate white flower. I zipped past, and then I noticed something happening on the ground. It seemed quite a few people were gathered wearing uniform yellow jackets, but then the next platform appeared, and I lost sight. I rang the bell and waited for Rob.

"Did you see the parrot?" He levered onto the stand.

"I did. Did you see all the people on the ground?"

He nodded. "I wonder what they were doing there. Ready? Last one."

I jumped.

Wind rushed past my face, and I relished it. I wondered if they have one of these near home. Jenny would love it.

The attendant was unstrapping me as Rob whisked onto the platform. "Too bad we don't have time to go again."

When we got to the parking lot, Sheila was pacing back and forth near twin buses. Becky and Sam stood to the side, talking in hushed voices as I approached. I said, "Wasn't that the best?"

"Randy fell."

"What?" My stomach lurched. Everything had seemed so solid, so safe. Randy was a big guy, but I didn't remember seeing a weight limit.

"I don't know what happened. They sent a team to get him."

Everyone faced the jungle, stony-faced. A few minutes later, Randy limped into the clearing, supported by two of the attendants. Sheila ran to him. "You're okay."

He hugged her and waved to the gathered crowd. "I'm good. Nothing to see here." People began to load onto the buses.

He limped our way, arm heavy around Sheila. Rob ran to assist, and Randy draped his other arm around him. They joined us, and Becky asked, "What happened? We were so scared when you didn't come out."

"Darndest thing. My strap gave way, and I plummeted. Luckily, I hit a bunch of branches and then landed on a bed of the biggest ferns I'd ever seen. Had the breath knocked out of me, got some pretty good scratches," he displayed the cuts on his arm, "and twisted my ankle, but it could have been far worse."

Sheila hugged him again. "Don't scare me like that."

The bus driver approached. "We need to leave for the pier. Do you want to go to the hospital? I can get someone to take you."

Randy shook his head. "Let's go back."

They boarded the bus, and I went to follow, but Rob touched my arm. "Ours is the other one. This must have been the earlier departure— that's why we didn't see the others before."

As the bus turned to leave, I saw Dawn and Michael in the third seat.

Rob and I boarded the other, now full bus and found seats in the back. I turned toward him. "Don't you think that's odd? The attendants were super careful to double-check everything. My harness was solid."

"He is a big guy." Rob shrugged. "Weight limit was two-seventy-five."

"You don't think he weighs more than that?"

"Could. Just seems suspicious, and you know how we feel about coincidences. Butch is dead, and Randy could've died today. Would have been convenient for Dawn if he had. Good thing for her she wasn't on the trip." He reached for my hand.

"But she was. Dawn and Michael were already on the bus. It wouldn't benefit Dawn, though. After last night's debacle, she didn't have to worry about Randy anymore. Plus, if Randy died, who would inherit his shares? Would it be Sheila or Becky?"

"I wonder how we could find out." Rob shut his eyes.

I poked him. "You're not going to believe this, but I'm hungry."

"Adrenaline will do that to you. Can you wait till we get back to the ship?"

"I guess I'll have to." My stomach growled.

"Because I love you." He handed me a candy bar from a side compartment in his camera bag.

"Want some?" I tore it open.

"Wouldn't deprive you." He kissed my nose.

I popped the last of it in my mouth and licked my fingers. "Thank you. Why did you have a snack squirreled away? I'm almost afraid to ask how old it was."

"Habits die hard. When I was a reporter overseas, we got caught in tough situations where eating was sporadic. Having a little something saved me on many an occasion."

We pulled up to the dock just after the other bus. The sun was high in the sky, and heat shimmered from the metal on the walkway. Michael and Dawn were at the bottom of the gangplank, handing their key cards to the ship's personnel, then there was another group of passengers, Sheila helping a limping Randy when one of the crew took over for her, and trailing was Becky and Sam, hand-in-hand, arms swinging.

"If Randy weren't limping, it'd seem like just another group coming back from a successful outing."

Chapter 12

Rob and I went back to the room to wash up. "One weird thing. Becky didn't seem all that upset. Randy is her only sibling, and now her parents are both dead. I would have thought she'd have been far more emotional. How would you have reacted if it were Elizabeth?" I hung up the towel.

"I would have been running through the jungle with the attendants." Rob donned a new t-shirt.

"Exactly. And what about Sheila? She was worried, sure, but not frantic. If it had been you..." My hands began to shake.

Rob pulled me to him. "It wasn't, and we had a terrific time. Focus on that." He frowned. "I wish we'd seen what order they were in."

"What do you mean?"

"Who was near Randy when he fell—who had opportunity?"

"Should we talk to the chief security officer? Tell him what we think?" I donned my wide-brimmed hat.

"As far as the ship is concerned, they think Butch died of natural causes, and this morning may have been a faulty harness, or Randy may have been too overweight for the zipline." Rob grabbed the bag with our beach stuff.

"But why would the harness have broken? Wouldn't the zipline have just snapped?"

He shrugged. "Could be either. At any rate, I'm not sure what we could tell him."

"And Dawn—Randy confessed to poisoning her. That's another thing." I opened the door to the room, and we exited.

"Okay. If it makes you feel better, we'll talk to him. Let's go to the reception desk and see if we can set up a meeting."

We traipsed the stairs to reception and told the man at the desk what we wanted. After asserting it was not an immediate concern, he told us he would relay the message and have Chief Security Officer Patterson meet us at the restaurant upstairs.

While walking to the other side of the ship, we stopped at the community games table to place puzzle pieces. It was one of those wooden ones with pretty yet devilish shapes. I picked up a piece that appeared to be an old-fashioned bicycle with an immense front wheel and snapped it into the correct place. The group we had seen last night had made good progress, so we had it easier. I could have stayed there all day finishing, but Rob said, "You had a snack. I'm hungry."

"Can't have that." I took his hand, and we jogged up the stairs to the restaurant. "Better sit at a table for four, so we have a seat for the security guy."

Rob pointed to one near the window, and I nodded. We placed our things and perused the buffet. That day's specialty was Indian food, and the centerpiece was chicken tikka masala. "Gotta love a ship that caters to many British passengers."

I added chana masala, saag paneer, and naan to my plate and sighed, "Your wife is one happy girl."

Rob opted for seafood and loaded his plate with shrimp, smoked trout, and marinated octopus. He eyed my plate and then added a few Indian delicacies to his.

We sat and dug in. "This is so good. My breath isn't going to be the greatest, but we're going to be in the same boat."

"Nothing a little mouthwash can't cure."

The sommelier arrived, and we went with the white wine he recommended, along with more water, to complete our feast.

Dawn sat with a full plate. "Hope you don't mind. This place is pretty crowded, plus I wanted to talk to you."

She turned to the sommelier. "Whatever they're having is fine with me."

"Uh." I didn't know how to get rid of her. Everyone had gotten back from their tours, so the restaurant was hopping. It would have been churlish to ask her to leave, but I was concerned the security officer might arrive while she was with us.

Dawn must have sensed my hesitation. "It's okay, isn't it?"

Rob waved his hand. "Happy to have you. What did you want to talk about?"

"This might be a bit awkward, so I'm just going to say it. I had you investigated." She speared an artichoke in her salad.

"Me?" Rob pointed to himself.

"Both of you. With all this craziness, I wanted to know who I was dealing with."

I guessed I could see her point, but I was kind of offended. They were crazy—we were just trying to enjoy our honeymoon. "And what did you find out?"

"You are who you say you are. And you've been known to help solve a few mysteries. There's a detective in your town," she glanced at her phone, "Ziebold, who is a big fan of both of you."

"A friend." Where was she going with this? "And?"

"To be frank, even though I would have been far happier if Butch hadn't died, things have gone relatively smoothly for me. I got control of the company I wanted. Randy was making some noise, but then he decided to poison me..." Dawn shuddered. "Anyway, I dealt with him, but now we have this unfortunate fall of his."

"Still don't get what this has to do with us." Rob sipped his drink.

"Maybe Randy just fell. Accidents happen. But if someone is targeting him, it would be hard to explain. I can't get off the ship and expect to run a business where both the owner and son died. Butch is explainable—he died of a heart attack. But both of them on the same trip? The publicity alone would kill me, to say nothing of what our board would think, and I've worked far too hard to achieve this." Dawn pushed her salad away and drank water. "So, I'd like to hire the two of you to figure out what's happening. We know you, so you'd be in a perfect position to help." She pushed a piece of paper toward us, and our eyes grew wide.

I stuttered, "We aren't private investigators. I'm an insurance agent, and Rob runs a newspaper. This isn't what we do."

Rob nodded. "Plus, there are only a few days left on the cruise. Once we dock, you'll be going back to New York, and we'll be returning to Hopeful."

"I have faith you'll be able to close this out before we dock." She rose. "Thanks for listening. I'll expect an answer later today." She turned and walked through the automatic doors.

"That's a lot of money." Rob picked up the paper and handed it to me. "It'd help with Jenny's tuition."

I stared at the amount. "Fifty thousand dollars. Is she trying to buy us off? Nobody pays that kind of money to two amateurs they don't know. Maybe she wants us in her pocket. Maybe she's trying to buy our silence." I shook my head. "She was very cold in how she talked about Butch's death. Maybe she killed him and is worried they'll open an investigation into what happened to Randy."

"A lot of maybes. You can't deny she made sense. The coincidence would be pretty bad." Rob took another sip of wine. "And you have solved a few cases."

"This is something we're going to need to think about. Are we even allowed to do this? We have no standing."

"Never stopped us before." He grinned.

Chief Security Officer Patterson stood in front of our table. "I heard you were trying to find me. I'm a little rushed today—would you mind if I got something to eat?"

"No problem."

He returned to the table with a full plate and sat. The waiter brought water and black coffee.

"I guess they know what you want here." I laughed.

"Perk of the job." He added dressing to the salad, and then he lifted his eyes. "Are you enjoying your cruise? Is this the first time with our line?"

"It's wonderful. Most of the cruisers we've talked with have been on multiple cruises with you. I can see why—the service is impeccable, and the food is wonderful. And I love the fact everything's included, so I don't have to worry about what I order." I leaned back in my chair.

"I'll pass along your comments, and I hope you become one of our loyal cruisers too. Now, why don't you tell me what's troubling you?"

Rob and I exchanged glances, and I said, "Rob, why don't you start."

He cleared his throat. "Chief Security Officer Patterson—"

"Bill, call me Bill."

"Bill, when Butch died, I told you I had seen a snake—"

"Didn't see it. It's unfortunate, but the guy died of a heart attack. His wife said he'd had one before..." He shrugged. "Sad, but it happens."

"Right." Rob leaned forward. "But then we had the poisoning of Ms. Franklin."

"Her son-in-law did that. Got his confession on the stage—one for the books. She decided not to press charges—said it was a prank gone wrong." Bill shook his head. "Should have charged him anyway."

"And now, Randy fell from the zip-line on tour today."

"Hadn't heard that. He must be okay, or I would have been informed." Bill took a bite of salad.

"Don't you think that's a lot to happen to one family on one cruise?" Rob asked.

"Coincidences do happen." He finished his coffee. "Anything else?"

"Dawn just asked us to look into things for her. Try to figure out what's going on," I said.

"Are you licensed private investigators?"

"Of course not. We don't even know if we want to help." Rob shrugged. "In fact, we don't even know if there's anything to help with."

"Our ship flies under the Bahamian flag. And similar to states within America, it has rules, regulations, and licensing requirements for someone holding themselves out as investigators."

Rob shrugged. "Guess we'll have to go back to the plan of tightening our boot laces to send Jenny to school."

"We were never going to take the money anyway." I poked his arm.

"I know. But it was good to dream."

Bill handed the waiter his empty salad plate and stood. "If there's nothing else?"

We shook our heads.

"Enjoy the rest of the cruise."

The lunch crowd had dissipated, but latecomers were still milling about at the buffet. Only one person was waiting at the gleaming, stainless steel ice cream station, and I was tempted for a moment. A simple dish of chocolate would hit the spot...

"What do you want to do?" Rob asked.

"Sorry, wool-gathering." I turned my attention back to him. "First, we turn Dawn down."

Rob pretended to wipe away a tear.

"And then we try to figure out what's going on. Like always."

Rob grinned and kissed my cheek.

"Why don't you get us set up by the pool, and I'll let the 'Merry Widow' know we won't be taking her up on her offer." I stood.

He went in the direction of the pool while I climbed the stairs to Dawn's suite. Arriving, I rang the bell, and the butler answered the door. "Ms. March, Ms. Franklin was hoping you'd drop by." He led me to the balcony, where Dawn and Michael lay on the double chaise lounge. Michael might have been snoozing, a baseball cap covering his face.

"Ms. March," the butler intoned.

"That was fast." Dawn swiveled to a sitting position. "Join us." She turned to the butler. "Lemonade, please."

"Very good." He left.

I moved to the other chaise and sat. "Not going to be here long. I wanted to tell you Rob and I are declining your offer. We are not licensed, private investigators."

"Who would know?" Dawn smiled. "I'm certainly not going to tell."

"It wouldn't be right." I crossed my legs. "So, we won't take you up on your offer."

The butler brought lemonade garnished with candied lemon peels.

"Delightful." I took a sip and smiled at him.

"Would madam like anything else?"

Dawn shook her head, and he withdrew. "Not going to lie—I'm disappointed," she said.

"I do have a question for Michael." I chewed on a piece of the peel—it was tart and sugary. "Yummy."

Michael lifted his hat. "Fire away. If I can answer, I will."

"If Dawn dies, what happens? Who gets the company?"

Dawn stared. "If you're not taking the job, why do you need to know?

"Curious."

Dawn nodded at Michael. "You can answer."

"Right now, her shares revert to Randy—Butch insisted. But we're working on changing her will and having him officially renounce the shares Butch left him—for remuneration, of course. Given everything that's happened, I don't think he'll walk away."

"What happens if Randy dies? Do the shares go to Sheila? Or Becky?" I traced the sweat beading on my glass.

"They split it. Half goes to Sheila, and half goes to Becky."

"Thanks for your candor." I rose and nodded to Dawn. "Sorry we couldn't help." She started to stand, and I said, "Don't get up. I can see my own way out." I strode from the suite and then down the stairs to the pool. Surveying the crowded deck, I texted Rob: "Where are you?"

"Thought you left me. Go toward the bar and then come forward a few rows."

I spotted him and headed in that direction. As soon as I sat down, a waiter appeared. "Something to drink?"

"Ice water please," I said.

"You were gone a long time." Rob kissed my hand.

"You're not going to believe what I found out." I lathered my face with sunscreen.

Rob pointed to the couple next to him and lifted his index finger to his lips.

Randy's eyes were shut, and his mouth sagged. His wrapped ankle was propped on towels topped by a bag of ice, and Sheila was in a red bikini on her stomach with a large straw hat covering her face.

My eyes widened, and then I nodded. I mouthed, "Why did you sit here?"

"Only place." He shrugged.

Randy snorted, and Sheila hit his bad leg. "Wake up."

"Ow. What'd you do that for?"

"You were snoring." She removed her hat. "Time for me to turn over, anyway." Her eyes widened as she saw us. "When did you two get here?"

"I scored these seats about an hour ago. Merry just got here."

"How is your ankle?" I asked Randy.

111

He wiggled his foot and grimaced. "Fine, as long as I don't move it too much. Good place to injure it. Pool, people to bring you drinks, yes, if it had to happen, this is not too bad."

"That was a tough fall. Could've been much worse," Rob said.

"I've become a big fan of ferns." Randy waved to the waiter. "Gin and tonic, extra lime."

The waiter turned to Sheila, "And for you?"

"Strawberry Daquiri."

Rob said, "Beer for me."

"More ice water would be great." I turned toward Randy. "It just seems weird that your harness would suddenly break. Didn't you check it? I did mine and had Rob test it—I was so scared of falling."

"Done it a dozen times. Those fellows know what they are doing." He paused. "Or at least I thought they did. I pulled on the straps a couple of times—seemed sturdy to me.

"Sheila's been on me about my weight—she says that's why I fell. Most limits are two-seventy-five." He patted his belly.

"That's what this one was," Rob said.

"I don't weigh near that much."

"Maybe pre-cruise." Sheila laughed.

Randy glared. "Not funny. You could have lost me."

"But I didn't." She caressed his hand. "And I'm pleased about that."

The assistant cruise director stopped at our chairs. "Pool volleyball in two minutes. Want to play? We're choosing sides."

"I'm out." Randy pointed to his ankle.

"Merry, you want to play?" Rob rose.

"Nope. I'm comfy here. Enjoy."

"I'll play." Sheila stood and walked with Rob to where the group was gathering.

There were a few ringers in the bunch, but most people seemed like vacation players out to have a good time. The entertainment crew worked to split the group evenly, and Sheila and Rob ended up on the same team. When play began, there was far more splashing going on than a ball going over the net. Rob made a diving save, and I applauded.

Play resumed, and Randy said, "You look like you want to join them—don't feel like you have to stay here with me."

"I'm fine watching. Can I ask you a question?"

He nodded.

"What order were you in before you fell? For us, I went first, and Rob followed."

Randy rubbed his chin. "That's tough. I know at the beginning, I went first, and Sheila was second. Michael and that tramp, Dawn, hadn't gone yet—I think they were right behind me. Then, on the platform after the first ride, we caught up with Becky and Sam, or they waited for us. Huh. I wonder why they did that—"

There was a scream from the pool, and I turned my head. One of the female players had gotten scratched by another and was creating quite a bit of drama. A member of the entertainment staff escorted her from the pool, cleaned the wound, and applied a band aid. Play resumed but seemed to be a bit less cut-throat.

"Sorry," I said, "Please continue."

"Anyway, I was the last to leave the platform, and Dawn had just arrived. I felt my strap snap about two hundred yards in, and I hurtled through the air." He paled. "I can tell you—I said a quick prayer." His face flushed. "It was scary. You know the rest, the people working there found me pretty quickly after they noticed I was missing."

"I can imagine." I shuddered. "Did anyone come close to you before that second ride?"

"You saw those platforms—they certainly aren't built for much more than two people at a time, and we had four. We were pretty crunched."

"Score!" Rob shouted, and his team cheered. The group exited the pool, and Rob and Sheila came back, laughing. He plopped next to me and wiped his face on a towel. "That was a workout—you should have come."

Sheila dried her hair and said, "It was fun."

"Sheila's a good player. She scored for us twice."

"Not as many times as you." Sheila fawned.

"If I could break up this mutual admiration society, I'd like to get back to the room and rest for a while." Randy gingerly got to his feet, favoring his one leg.

"You were sleeping here. How much rest do you need?" Sheila grumbled as she put their things in a beach bag and stood. "Nice game, partner." She patted Rob on the shoulder and left with Randy.

"I think you have a new admirer," I chided.

Rob leaned back on the chaise and put his hands behind his head. "So many I hardly know what to do with them all."

"But I'm the only one you reciprocate with, right?"

He pulled me close. "You bet."

"Well, while you were cavorting in the pool, I've been hard at work."

He kissed me. "Do tell."

Chapter 13

R ob called from the bathroom as he straightened his tie. "How'd we get invited to the captain's table anyway?"

I rounded the corner, and he looked me up and down. I was wearing a short blush sundress that clung to my curves and had tamed my unruly red tresses by inserting two turquoise clips.

"Do we need to eat? I'd rather stay here." He nuzzled my neck.

I gave him an air kiss. "Not spoiling my makeup. And on the invite, I have no idea. Our travel agent? Maybe your mother and Mac? At any rate, it should be fun."

Rob donned his suit jacket as I lifted my purse and stuck my key card inside. He opened the door for me, and we headed to the restaurant. I slipped my arm through his just before we got to the reception area. "Do you think they have a different menu for that table?"

"No idea. I hope he's a fun guy."

The Maître D' led us to a large round table for eight at the center of the restaurant, which featured a lovely arrangement of tea roses, stephanotis, and trailing sweet pea. We were the first to arrive, and the waiters held our chairs.

"I wonder who the others are," I murmured to Rob.

"Oh no." He stared at the entrance.

Becky and Sam were being led our way. Rob stood as they arrived at our table. "Ladies."

Sam sat next to Rob, and Becky sat next to her.

Becky said, "We keep running into you."

"Our luck," Rob quipped.

The captain arrived and sat next to me. He was an attractive, trim Italian man. We introduced ourselves, but he seemed to be already familiar with our story and congratulated us on our wedding and Becky and Sam on their engagement. Michael and Dawn joined us as we chatted about our experiences on the cruise. Dawn sat on the other side of the captain, and Michael was next to her. My stomach clenched. *Surely, they wouldn't have Randy at the table. Not after last night. The captain might not be aware, but someone on the ship would have changed the arrangements. Wait, there's only one empty chair. Is Sheila coming and not Randy?* A moment later, the hotel manager joined us, and I breathed a sigh of relief.

Rob asked, "Captain, I'd love to see the bridge. Do you give tours?"

"Tonight, we are all good friends sharing a meal—please call me Antonio. And, of course, we do have tours." He addressed the hotel manager, "Will you let the front desk know?" and then turned to us. "Tomorrow at 11? It's a sea day, so we should have time. Check-in with them in the morning."

The other people at the table chimed in, "We'd like to go too."

"Not a problem." The hotel manager smiled and made a note.

"Has anyone been to Italy?" Antonio asked. "I come from a little town outside of Firenze, or Florence as you call it in America. It's the most beautiful place in the world."

"I love the way the warm sun hits the buildings—that orange glow. And having red wine in the open cafes. Oh, and the olives..." Dawn's voice broke. "Butch and I were there in September. It was gorgeous; we had such a lovely time."

"The cruise line extends its sympathies," Antonio murmured.

"The flowers that were delivered to the room were exquisite. I appreciated your thoughtfulness." She seemed to pull herself together. "Let's not be sad tonight. It's one of our last nights on the ship."

Sam asked Becky, "What are you getting?"

Antonio lifted his hand, "I encourage you to try a special degustation menu that the chef prepared for us tonight, and as a special treat, the sommelier and I collaborated this afternoon on pairing it with Italian wines."

I handed Rob my menu. "I'm game."

"Me too." Rob closed his.

The waiter collected the menus, and the sommelier poured the first wine. It was a light red with notes of cherry and clove. When everyone had a glass, she said, "This is a Cianorie from the Fruili-Venezia Guilia region, near Slovenia."

Waiters brought two large serving dishes with selections of prosciutto-wrapped asparagus, beef carpaccio, shrimp, and pickled calamari. We passed the dishes, and I chose one of each of the items. The light, fruity taste of the wine worked perfectly with the food, and the table became quiet as everyone savored.

I wondered if we were destined to eat in silence and desperately tried to figure out a safe topic for discussion. "This wine works perfectly with the antipasto."

"Mm-hmm." There seemed to be general agreement around the table.

Surely one of us eight could figure out something innocuous to talk about. I turned to the captain. "What's your next voyage after this one?"

He put down his fork. "The western Caribbean. It has a flavor all its own. And we're heading into the holiday season." He smiled. "I'll tell you a secret—it's my favorite time of year to be at the helm. The hotel manager's team does a wonderful job decorating and getting into the spirit. It also seems like cruisers form deeper bonds over the holidays— everyone seems to take it slower and be more appreciative."

The hotel manager nodded.

"But don't you miss your families?" I asked. "I've only been gone a little over a week, but I lost a Thanksgiving with my daughter."

"But you had it with your new husband." Rob chided. "That should count for something."

I lifted his hand and kissed it. "It does, but you know what I mean."

"I do. But now we're talking about Christmas."

The hotel manager said, "We miss our families and our friends. However, people in this business love people, and it's such a joyful time it almost makes up for being away. But it also means we treasure our time with our loved ones that much more."

The next course was served with another wine, this time a deeper red. Becky said, "I wish I had brought my oils and easel. I would have loved to paint on the balcony."

"Even though I have no doubt any picture would have been beautiful, I'd hate to think of lugging all that stuff with us." Sam gave a pretend shudder.

Becky elbowed her. "Maybe if someone didn't bring so many shoes."

"What can I say? I like to have choices."

"Good thing that NFT sold. I guess you can buy another pair now." Becky took a sip of wine. "This is luscious."

"NFT?" Rob asked.

"Non-fungible Token. I started playing around with digital art, and it's taken off. I've sold quite a few."

I leaned forward. "I'm going to need more explanation. What is it, and why would I want to buy one?"

"I'm surprised you even know about them," Dawn sniffed. "After all, finance isn't your thing."

Sam bristled, and Becky put a hand on her shoulder. Becky handed me her phone. "Here's one of my pieces." It was an abstract piece of a mist-covered meadow.

"It's beautiful," I said.

"Thanks. It just sold to a collector in Atlanta."

"Is that the price?" I gasped.

She smiled.

"So, then you package up the piece and ship it to the buyer?" Rob asked.

"Nope. They own the original digital version."

"So, they could print it and hang it on a wall?" I took a roll from the basket.

"If they wanted." She smiled. "The point is that they own something unique from the artist."

"Too deep for me." I shook my head.

"You should hear what she's done in Bitcoin investing. She made a killing by getting in while it was hot and getting out before it sank. She inherited Butch's way with money." Sam beamed at Becky and then turned to Dawn. "Butch never realized how talented Becky was, being his second child and a girl. His loss. She's super creative and a financial wiz."

"I never realized…" Dawn's neck reddened.

"If he were smart, he would have left her the company."

Becky put her hand over Sam's. "Enough about me."

The main course of osso buco arrived, and the aroma of rosemary, thyme, and cloves enveloped the table. Antonio said, "This is one of my favorites—the chef simmers it for hours until it almost falls off the bone."

The sommelier poured wine into new wider-mouthed glasses. "This is a Barolo from the Piedmont region of Italy."

I sipped the wine after a bite of the veal and almost swooned. "This is delicious."

"Best thing I've ever had," Michael said.

I had almost forgotten he was there, he had been so silent. He and Dawn had been sharing the same chaise earlier in the day. I wondered if they were moving their relationship, if there was one, to a new level, and I also pondered how Sheila felt about that.

Rob nudged my foot under the table and mouthed, "What's wrong."

I shook my head and resumed eating as the table grew quiet, with people savoring their meal. After everyone seemed to be finished, I turned to the hotel manager. "When do you start decorating for Christmas?"

"As soon as this cruise docks. It'll be hectic, but while the luggage is being taken off the boat, we'll start in the closed dining rooms and move our way to the public areas as our guests leave us."

"Sounds like you'll be busy." Rob took a last bite of the veal and pushed his plate away.

"Um," Becky broke in, "Since we're back on Christmas again, I'd like to ask you something, Dawn. We've been talking about having our wedding then." Becky clutched Sam's hand. "I know this is sudden, but we'd love to have it at the house. Do you think that's possible? I texted Pastor Denise, and she has availability on the twenty-third."

Dawn was mid-sip and almost dropped the wine glass. "Might not work."

"I told you she'd say that," Becky said to Sam, "with Dad dead, we won't be welcome anymore."

"That's not it—I'm in talks to sell the house. I'll be out of the house a week before Christmas if the deal goes through. I meant to tell you about it when we got back."

Becky stood. "You've already got a buyer? When did that happen? Dad didn't tell me you were selling the house." She turned to Michael. "This is all your doing. You shady..." She turned on her heel and left the room.

"It's just that this is all a bit sudden." Sam got to her feet and followed Becky.

Dawn lifted her water glass. "I'm sorry we have these very public breakdowns. Everyone is under quite a bit of stress."

Antonio and the hotel manager excused themselves after thanking us for joining them, and the waiter brought tiramisu. I took a bite. The flavor of coffee was prominent, and it almost seemed like they had put custard between the delicate layers of cake. I sighed. "I have to stop eating, but this is so good."

"I know the sale seems sudden." Dawn squirmed. "It's a hot market right now, and the place is oceanfront. But way too big." Dawn scrolled on her phone and handed it to me. The picture was of a sprawling cape with a slate roof, weathered gray shingles, and about ten thousand square feet of living space. Then, she swiped right to a dramatic view of a promontory overlooking dashing waves.

"I can see why they'd want to be married there. Such a beautiful backdrop," Rob said.

"Becky's mother bought the place a few years before disappearing." Dawn sighed. "If I'd been thinking, I should have offered the apartment in Manhattan or the mountain place in Vermont. I'll call them when I get back to the room. It wouldn't be good if Becky and Randy both weren't speaking to me when I meet with the board next month."

The sommelier tried to tempt us with Limoncello, but we passed on it. I felt like Rob would have to roll me to the room as it was.

Chapter 14

As soon as we walked in, I opened the desk drawer and lifted the pad of paper and pen. "We need to make a list. It's gotten to the point where I can't keep everything straight."

"Good idea. But I think better in more comfortable clothes." Rob changed into a pair of shorts and t-shirt, and I followed his example. "Let's do this on the deck—make sure you hold onto the paper—they were talking about it getting rough a bit later."

"Got it."

He yanked the door open, and we sat at the table. I plopped the pad onto it and began to write under the header, "Motive to kill Butch."

"Let's talk about Dawn first—why would she have wanted to kill him?" I jotted money and power.

"He didn't treat her well—we saw that."

"Wouldn't someone just get divorced if they felt they were ill-used?" I asked.

Rob pointed at what I had written. "Not if their goal was money and power. Who knows? If they had a prenup, she might not have gotten anything on divorce. And, speaking of which—what about the Michael thing—maybe she wanted to get rid of Butch because of a new love?"

"I'm still on the fence on that one, but let's write it down."

"What about Randy? What would his motive have been?" Rob picked up a pencil, took the pad, and wrote. "Company—he definitely was interested in taking over for his father. Maybe payback? We saw them arguing the day we got on the boat—he could've been tired of being underestimated and wanted to run it for himself."

"Would he kill his father because Butch didn't respect his contributions? I could see him doing it for the company—it's worth a lot, but for esteem? Seems a bit extreme."

"Stranger things have happened." Rob pointed out.

"Leave it there. You could be right. But put money as a motive for him as well."

Rob added it. "Let's do Sheila next."

"She likes to treat herself. It may be that Randy wasn't making enough. She might have wanted more money and thought that he would inherit. After all, Becky wasn't involved in the company, and Butch and Dawn hadn't been married that long. It's not a stretch to think that Randy would have gotten the bulk of it." I stood. "Want water?"

Rob nodded. I retrieved the large bottle the steward had tucked into the refrigerator and poured water into our reusable containers. When I returned, Rob was writing Becky's name on the pad.

"Becky's interesting." I handed him the aluminum bottle.

"How so?" He took a sip.

"On one hand, she seems happy being an artist. On the other, she seems bitter that she was not seen as "finance material." Like she wasn't smart enough to be part of the business. You heard her at dinner—it sounds like she's been doing well with her and Sam's money—and seems up to date on new investment schemes."

"Not investments I'd be comfortable with." Rob shuddered.

"Me neither. I'm much less of a risk-taker. What about Sam?"

He wrote her name. "I think we have to put money under their names as well. It's got to be expensive to run a gallery. We don't know how well it was doing."

"We also don't know that they were making a good return on their investments—we only have their word on that. You need to add marriage too. They hadn't been able to get engaged while Butch was alive. That seems like a good motive."

Rob added it. "What about Michael?"

"Not sure. It doesn't seem like he had much to gain except for a bunch more work. But maybe if he was in love with Dawn and wanted Butch out of the way..." I rubbed the back of my neck. "That works only if he didn't care about the money or company. Hmm. What if it were the other way around, and Dawn was using him? What if she got closer to find out what was in the will—nope—it doesn't work. If that were true, she would think that Randy would inherit since he didn't know the will had been changed, and there would be no benefit to killing Butch."

Rob pointed at Sheila's name. "What was going on with Sheila and Michael? From what you said, they were close at tea the other day. Was Michael hedging his bets? Or was Sheila the one trying to worm information out of him?"

The wind picked up, and my hair blew around my face. Rob held the pad so it couldn't cartwheel off the table and over the railing into the water below. He asked, "Want to go in?"

I shook my head. "It's nice and warm—but I think I will put clips in my hair so I can see. I'll be right back." I stood, and the sliding door to the room next to us slammed shut.

My mouth dropped. "I didn't know anyone was there—did you hear anything?"

"Not until the door shut."

"Do you think they could hear us?"

"The waves are pretty loud, and the wind picked up."

"But only just."

"Dawn's on fourteen, so it can't be her. Not sure where Sam and Becky are." I frowned. "Randy and Sheila are on this floor, but they're in nine-fifty. I wonder where Michael's room is?"

"It's probably someone who got bored listening to us." Rob shrugged.

"But if that is Michael's room, it could have been him or Dawn." I bit my lip.

"Or it could have been Sheila. They were pretty cozy."

"In any event, I think from now on, we should have these conversations inside."

He held the door for me, and I slid past. Once the door was shut, Rob pulled me into his arms. "We need to be more careful. And speaking of which, I don't want you traipsing about the ship on your own anymore."

"I told Dawn we weren't investigating. Shouldn't we be safe?"

Rob frowned. "We've been thrown in with these people and have been exposed to a lot of their dirty laundry. I'd feel better if we erred on the cautious side—it's only a few more days. We're on a ship with a heck of a lot of ocean around, and people have been known to disappear."

"Aye, aye, captain." I saluted.

"Merry, I'm serious."

I kissed him. "I know. I'll try." I sat on the bed and patted the space next to me. "Now, what's our next step?"

"I'll try to find out more about the gallery. I need to check on the paper, anyway."

"I'm going to see what I can find out about Michael. He seems to be a linchpin."

Rob's eyebrow rose. "And how are you going to do that and stay safe?"

"Online—and in the same room as you. There's more than one computer there, you know." I stood. "And now, my dear husband, it's time for bed."

❋ ❋ ❋

Rob pushed back his chair in the library. "I've uploaded my freelancer's pictures from the firehouse Thanksgiving event. Want to see?"

125

I stood and rounded the desk to stand behind Rob. He had a few great shots of the serving line, the firefighters helping the kids climb on the truck, and the guests eating at long tables. "Isn't that Ed and Andy at the end of the table? What were they doing there?"

Rob showed another picture of Ed proudly carving an immense, beautifully browned, glistening textbook-perfect turkey. "They volunteered."

"That was nice of them. Plus, once people try the food, they'll have to stop by their café."

Rob saved his file. "Now, on to the gallery. What was the name of it?"

I leaned forward. "A Bevvy of Art and Design."

"Bevvy?"

"Named for Becky's mom, Bev. Clever."

Rob tapped on the keyboard.

"I guess I should stop doing actual work and try to learn more about Michael." I sank back into my seat across from him.

"You know that Cheryl has everything well in hand."

I nodded. "I just feel guilty piling everything on her shoulders."

"She's just the general. Don't worry—she's not doing it all herself—you have other staff." He checked his watch. "We have about thirty minutes before we need to be downstairs for the tour. I suggest we make the most of it."

I logged off work, opened one of the social media sites, and typed Michael's name. "I never know why people don't check privacy settings. I can see all of his pictures."

"Anything interesting?"

"Checking."

"Speaking of which..." Rob rose and wandered around the library.

"What are you doing?"

"Wanted to make sure we were alone."

"Good idea." I nodded.

He resumed scrolling as I searched through Michael's photo history. "He has a taste for the high life, that's for sure." There were numerous pictures of him with other men in their late twenties-early thirties, drinking something like whiskey and smoking cigars. "Yuck. Why do men think it's a good thing to smoke?"

"Not all men." Rob pointed to his chest.

"I stand corrected." I moved further back. "Not a lot of pictures of women... Wait a minute." There was an early picture of Michael at some kind of prom, and his date looked very familiar. "Rob, take a gander."

He moved to my side of the desk.

I pointed. "Do you recognize her?"

"A very young Sheila. Maybe sixteen?"

"She didn't mention they were old friends." I frowned.

"I'm not sure how that would have come up in conversation. We didn't ask them how they knew each other—we just assumed it was because he was Butch's lawyer." Rob's phone alarm went off. "We'll have to continue this later. Don't forget to wipe your browsing history."

I did that and stood. "Still seems kind of curious. Were you able to find out anything about the gallery?"

"Listed as one to watch, and it's gotten a lot of favorable press. I'll examine it more later."

We jogged the showcase wooden tile stairs to the reception area, a wide-open space with plenty of comfy tan and brown-trimmed high-backed chairs and sofas arranged in various conversational areas. Becky and Sam were seated on a couch near the desk and, as Sam waved us over, she said, "They told us to wait here."

I sat next to them, and Rob took a chair opposite. "Are we it?" I asked.

"The others are just slow. Dawn called me last night to offer up the other houses for the wedding, and she said she'd be here this morning." Becky tossed a glance over her shoulder.

"Are you going to take her up on it?" I lifted one of the ship's flyers from the table next to me and flipped through it, not wanting to appear too interested.

Sam sighed. "We haven't decided. The beach would have been great. Most of our friends are on the east coast, so the mountain place is out. Maybe Manhattan."

"It was nice of her to offer, but it still makes me mad she's selling the place. It was my mom's. I don't know why Dad left it to Dawn. He should have given it to Randy or me. She could have gotten the other properties." Becky grumbled.

Sam said, "Maybe we should make her an offer."

"I'm not paying for a house that should have been mine."

"If you want it..." Sam shrugged.

"Sounds like it's a done deal anyway." Becky put her arm around Sam. "But thanks for suggesting it."

Sheila approached from the coffee bar. "I heard there was a tour."

"Going to see the bridge," Rob said.

"Sounds like fun."

Sam pointed toward reception. "I think you need to register."

"What are they going to do, say we can't go? We're family." Sheila sank onto the chair next to Rob.

Michael and Dawn rounded the corner from the shops, walked to the desk, and handed them their packages. Then, they joined us.

Becky asked, "What did you buy?"

"Just some trinkets. The butler's going to put them in the room." Dawn dragged a chair from another grouping and sat.

Randy limped toward us, coffee in hand, and said to Sheila, "I turned around, and you were gone."

"Going on the bridge tour with them."

"Mind if I join?" Randy asked.

Dawn turned away but didn't say anything.

Becky asked, "Sure your ankle is up to it?"

"Long as we go slow." Randy eased into a chair.

A woman in a white uniform approached. "Is this everyone?"

"I think so." Rob stood, and we got to our feet.

"Follow me." She took us back up the stairs toward the library, and in the far corner was a non-descript door I hadn't noticed before. Randy caught up as she keyed in a code, and it opened to a large hallway with several other doors. One had a name tag for the chief engineer and then another labeled for the captain.

I mouthed to Rob, "Would love to see in there."

He nodded.

The guide continued forward and gave various stats—the ship's tonnage—fifty-five thousand—and number of passengers—eight hundred.

The captain and officer of the watch were deep in conversation about a crew drill the following day. Captain Antonio seemed displeased that it had been moved to a sea day when all the passengers were on board, and the officer of the watch was in the middle of an explanation that the delay was due to some type of mechanical issue when we approached. Their conversation broke off, and the guide introduced us to them both—Captain Antonio smiled and told her that he had met us the previous night.

Randy sniffed, "I wasn't at dinner last night, so it's nice to meet you." He shook the captain's hand. "Mind if I sit? Bum ankle." Randy perched on a chair.

I wandered from the group and pointed to a portion of the bridge that jutted from the ship, where the floor was a sheet of glass with a great view of the ocean below. "This is scary—what's it for?"

The captain turned away from Randy and walked to where I was standing. Then he leaped onto the glass. I flinched, expecting him to break through to the rushing sea below or at least see spiderweb-like cracks. "Don't worry. I keep trim so it won't break." He laughed. "Just kidding. It's quite safe and solid.

"It's so I can see the docks when we come into port. There are ones on both sides of the ship, which, as you can imagine, comes in quite handy. Now, if you walk back over here..." He led the group to an immense dashboard with dozens of lights and switches that could have come from the Starship Enterprise. There were roundish joystick controllers and monitors displaying most of the ship's outside. "As you can see, the boat is large, and we want to make sure we don't hit anything."

He explained how the automatic controls worked, the tiny steering wheel for use when approaching port, and what the various knobs controlled.

"Have you ever had anyone go overboard?" Randy interrupted him.

"During rough seas, you mean?" The captain asked for clarification.

"Could be. Or when it's calm. Either," Randy said

I squeezed Rob's hand. Everyone's faces had grown tense, and Sheila's face was pinched like she'd just downed a lemon.

"Randy, we don't need to talk about that," Dawn said. "I'd much rather learn about what happens when the port pilot comes on board." She turned to Captain Antonio. "How do you feel about turning your ship over to a pilot?"

"Except in very tricky ports, the pilot doesn't take over—they provide advice on the bridge. After all, they don't want to be responsible for a problem with a six-hundred-million-dollar ship. Miami is one where—"

"I'd like an answer to my question." Randy's face had grown red. Sheila put her hand on his arm, and he batted it away. "It's simple—just a yes or no."

The captain's face grew grim. "It has happened on rare occasions. I'm sure you've read about it. Not on this ship, thank goodness.

Sometimes seas are rough, and people don't pay attention. Other times..."

The guide jumped in, "If there are no other questions, this concludes our tour for today. Thank you for choosing our cruise line— we appreciate your patronage."

She left us in the library. Becky walked up to her brother and said, "You always ruin everything," then she turned on her heel and stalked out the door with Sam trailing after her.

Dawn just shook her head and left. Michael hesitated like he was going to say something but then decided against it.

Sheila grabbed Randy's arm. "Come on. Let's go get something to drink."

"It was just a question. I don't see what everyone's so upset about. I saw this show..."

Sheila pulled his hand and led him from the room.

Michael perused the book titles, grabbed one, and walked out.

I sank onto one of the chairs. "Alone at last. What do you think that was all about?"

"I don't know, but it reinforces that we must be careful. It also makes me grateful he wasn't at dinner last night."

"Me too. It was almost enjoyable—that is until Becky asked about using the house for her wedding." I shook my head. "What now?"

"We're in the library. I'm not that hungry yet—should we get back to work?"

"Let's."

He sat across from me at another computer. I had just pulled up Michael's social media again when Rob called me over. "You have to see this gallery. It's really something."

I brought my chair back around and sat as he pulled up the virtual tour on their website. It was in an old brownstone with twenty-foot ceilings, and the interior had been painted a matte black, which made the deeply saturated colors of Becky's art pop. Lighting was carefully angled to call attention to her brushwork.

"I wonder if that one's for sale. I love it." I pointed to an exuberant oil abstract painting that captured the essence of an ocean coming alive.

"What are you doing?" Michael demanded.

Rob and I jumped.

He was standing next to the computer I had been using, which was still on his social media page.

I felt my face grow hot, and Rob quickly shut down the computer he had been using.

"Were you checking up on me?"

Rob cleared his throat. "Hazard of the trade. I'm a reporter, so I always want to know more about the people I'm around. Didn't hear you come in."

"Wasn't fond of the book I selected, so I came for another." He lifted the hardback. "If you were interested, you could have asked."

"I didn't know you and Sheila knew each other." I walked to the computer and scrolled to the prom photo.

"We go way back. Our families were friends, and we spent a lot of vacations together. Nothing to hide."

"You broke up?" Rob asked.

"Obviously." Michael huffed. "Just stupid kid stuff to please the parents. Neither of us was serious. So, if you're done with your intrusive questions, I think I'll go." He slammed the book down, grabbed another, and left.

Rob groaned. "We have to be more careful."

"Good idea."

Chapter 15

We made our way across the pool deck, and Rob hesitated as we got to a sign by the grill. People lined up for the steaming dishes displayed under heat lamps on both sides. He said, "Seafood buffet today. Lobster, clams, shrimp, you name it. What do you think?"

"Sounds wonderful, but let's go to the casual restaurant in the back."

His mouth dropped. "Merry March turning down a seafood feast?"

"No tables for two here, and I don't want to take the chance of anyone joining us." I pointed to the seating area.

"Good point. I'm sure the food will be just as delicious there."

The automatic doors opened, and we strolled into the other eatery. I led the way to a white linen-draped table next to the windows and sat. Rob took off his hat and sunglasses and laid them on the table's edge, then joined me. A waiter appeared. "Something to drink?"

"Iced tea for me," I said.

"Same, thanks," Rob added.

We both stood and wandered to the buffet tables. They had wraps and sandwiches, a table with cold mussels, shrimp, and ceviche, as well as a hot buffet featuring Angus prime rib, mashed potatoes, and green beans, and a station with orecchiette, sausage, and eggplant.

Rob piled his plate at the seafood station, and I opted for the pasta, then took a small plate to the salad bar. When I rejoined him, he popped the last shrimp into his mouth. I said, "You must have been hungry."

He smiled. "Everything is so good. Plus, unpleasant mornings mean I need to have a hearty lunch. Be right back. There's a slice of prime rib with my name on it."

"At least get salad to go with it."

"A nagging wife, just what I always wanted." He kissed me on the cheek.

"Better believe it." I popped a marinated artichoke into my mouth.

Rob returned at the same time my pasta arrived at the table. I was happy to note he had followed my lead and added greens to accompany the slab of beef and gravy on his plate.

He eyed my bowl and said, "That looks good."

I spooned a sample onto a bread dish and handed it over.

"I wasn't suggesting—but I'll gladly take it off your hands." He laughed.

"What do you think Randy was driving at with his question?" I speared a piece of sausage.

"This is like butter," Rob said as he savored the roast. He cut me a sliver and passed me his fork.

"It really is lovely." I swallowed. "Back to Randy."

"Do we have to?"

"Not that much time left."

"I don't know why he asked that question. If he were thinking of sending someone overboard, I would think you wouldn't want to broadcast it by alerting everyone, including the ship's captain."

"Maybe he did see a show about it. It could've been idle curiosity." I moaned—the eggplant was divine.

Rob put his fork down. "Or, he could have been putting someone on notice."

"Huh?"

"Threatening them."

I blanched. "Would the person know? What if it was directed at us?"

"Seemed too pointed. Too ham-handed." Rob sliced another piece of beef and said, "Yep. Think he was threatening someone versus planning on it. And as to why not us, my dear wife, we don't have anything he wants."

A school of dolphins frolicked in the ship's wake, and people who had been milling about getting food swarmed toward our side to take in the sight. Becky and Sam were part of the group.

Sam poked Rob's shoulder. "You have a front-row seat."

He smiled. "That we do."

She pointed to an empty table a few feet away. "Will we cramp your style if we sit here?"

"Have at it." I smiled halfheartedly. *That's the end of that conversation.*

Rob and I gazed out the window, watching the dolphins at play. He reached across the table and held my hand. "Now, this is how I envisioned our honeymoon. Good food, great nature, and fabulous wife."

I grinned. "I love you, Rob."

"Tell me the truth." Dawn was suddenly next to our table, her color was high, and her voice was louder than I would have liked it to be.

"Did someone else hire you? Michael said you've been investigating him. Are you checking my background too?"

"What?" My mouth gaped like one of the fish chasing the dolphins we had been watching.

"Why are you researching us? I was trying to hire you for the others."

Becky threw her napkin onto their table, stood, and got toe-to-toe with Dawn. "You hired them to investigate us?"

I guessed Dawn had been so intent on Rob and me she hadn't noticed Becky and Sam sitting there, though it would have been hard for her to miss the crowd watching the dolphins who had turned their attention toward us.

Dawn said more softly, "Not you per se. Just in general. I thought there was something fishy about your father's death."

"Nothing strange about it. Just a way too young for him wife, who inherited the lion's share of his estate." Becky's voice rose as she played to the crowd. "Who would be more likely to have caused my father's death? The now-rich widow? Or his kids? I'm voting her."

The Maitre D' appeared, and several waiters came with him. The servers ushered the crowd back to their seats while the Maitre D' said, "Ladies. I must ask you to stop. I can't have this kind of disturbance in my restaurant."

Becky sputtered. "She started it."

"I'm going." Dawn pivoted on her heal and left.

Sam moved to Becky's side and glared at Rob. "I can't believe you were trying to help her. I thought we were friends." She put her arm around Becky. "Let's go."

"I guess they all know we're working on this now." My hands were shaking.

Rob's face was grim. "Sure seems that way. On the other hand, we might finally get alone time, except for Randy and Sheila."

"I give them ten minutes before Becky lets them know." I had been planning on a scoop of ice cream for dessert, but my churning stomach said no.

After lunch, we returned to the room, and I picked up the pad we had been working on the night before. "Let's examine this again. Have we learned anything new?"

Rob lifted it and sat in the desk chair while I peered over his shoulder from the bed. He tapped the Michael header. "He admitted he and Sheila were close friends."

I frowned. "He didn't exactly say they were friends. More that their families threw them together."

"If they vacationed together and dated as kids, I would think they'd know all there is to know about each other. And I think Sheila rubbing his leg at tea would indicate they are still, at least, he air-quoted 'friends.'"

"Good point. We also know Michael and Dawn are talking about more than business, since he told her we had his social media page up."

Rob nodded. "Plus, we found out Randy either is threatening someone, wants to throw someone overboard, or saw a strange show to be watching before going on a cruise."

"Which leaves us... Nowhere." I rubbed the back of my neck.

He got up and sat next to me. "Tense?"

"Uh-huh."

"It's frustrating, but we really don't know these people, and we'll be leaving the boat soon." He massaged my shoulders.

"Being on this ship is like living in a small town, running into everyone all the time and knowing everyone's business." I lifted Rob's hand from my neck. "I think something happened, and we wouldn't be the people I know we are if we let the guilty person just waltz away—we can't let that person get away with it." I paused. "Are you a betting man?"

"Why?"

"Who would you put your money on?"

"The wife. She inherited the lion's share and is leaving the boat in a far better position than when she got on."

"But what about what happened on the rafting trip? Something hit her." I poured myself a glass of water.

"She had a scratch on her forehead. It's kind of suspicious she ended up floating face-up. She could have done it to herself." He paused. "Who do you think did it?"

"Haven't decided yet. It usually is the spouse, so you could be right."

"What's next?"

"A nap. And then we try to find out more about our suspects."

* * *

I parted the curtains to a sky of slate gray, and lightning flashed in the distance as waves dashed against the ship. "We're in for a rocky time this afternoon. Hopefully, it'll calm down in time for dinner."

"Guess we won't have any pool time today."

I shook my head. "And the library may be crowded, so continuing to research may not pan out."

"There's an art auction in twenty minutes. I know Becky and Sam didn't think it was high quality, but it might be fun."

"Let's go."

Chairs had been set up auditorium style in one of the lounges we had yet to try. Artwork stood on easels two deep in a rectangle, surrounding the room. As soon as we entered, there was a registration table to our right, and an art gallery employee urged us to sign in to get a paddle. Rob glanced at me, and I shook my head and said to the woman, "We'll browse, and if we see something we like, we'll be back."

A tuxedoed gentleman handed us each a glass of champagne, and we joined the crowd touring the room. Rob whispered, "There aren't any prices. How are we supposed to know what's a good deal or not? You'd think they'd at least have a reserve price."

"Maybe we were supposed to have researched before we came." I spotted Becky and Sam across the room. "Surprised to see them here. Too bad about that tiff after lunch. We could've asked for their opinions."

Rob crossed the room to where they were standing. I gawked for a moment, wondering what he was doing, and then followed. He said, "Sam, let me explain."

"Fine. Go ahead." Her lips formed a thin line.

The loudspeaker blared. "There will be a crew drill in fifteen minutes. We would appreciate if passengers would please keep clear of the stairways during the drill and avoid the watertight doors."

"How are we supposed to know which ones are watertight?" I asked.

"The ones with the rubber gaskets and rounded edges." Rob tossed back over his shoulder and then moved his attention back to Sam and Becky. "Dawn did try to hire us to uncover what happened to your father. She wasn't satisfied with the heart attack explanation—but we turned her down. We're not private eyes."

"That doesn't even make sense," Sam said. "Why would Dawn think you two knew anything about investigating a murder?"

"Um." I cleared my throat. "She ordered a report on us and discovered we helped our local police solve a few of them."

Becky gave a bitter laugh. "So, she was investigating you while you were investigating us. Michael mentioned you were going through his social media. Did you investigate us too?"

"Just your gallery," Rob said. "Your work is amazing."

"Thanks. But if you turned Dawn down, why do you care?"

"Curious." Rob shrugged. "As I told Michael, it's a hazard of the profession. I just wanted to know what happened to your father."

"Heart attack. Plain and simple. Too much whiskey, food, and not enough exercise. His doctor had been after him for years. My father made money, but he liked to spend it on creature comforts too. Hence his wife." Becky's mouth twisted.

"I guess fair's fair. Dawn intruded on your life, so you intruded on ours. And if we want to see the auction, we ought to grab seats." Sam studied our empty hands. "No paddle?"

"Not sure what to bid on," I said.

Becky took an aisle seat near the back, and Sam sat next to her, then Rob and me. The auctioneer began his spiel and, to get the crowd excited, said, "If you check under your chair, you may find something interesting."

Everyone immediately bent over to feel under their seats, and various cries sprung up from people who found a piece of paper. Becky got one from her chair and handed it to Rob. "In case you decide to get in on the action. I'm not going to bid on this dreck."

It was a certificate for one hundred dollars off an item purchased in the auction. "A hundred? Wow, these things must be very expensive."

Becky rolled her eyes. "And way more than they're worth."

There was another announcement from the bridge. "The crew drill has commenced. Thank you."

The bidding began, and Becky whispered to Sam and left. Rob asked, "Where's she going?"

"Needed air. She's going up on deck."

"Is that safe? The waves were getting pretty high, and the wind was whipping."

"She'll come back, or I'll go up after a few minutes. I've never been to one of these at sea and want to see how they get people to buy—maybe there's a trick or two I can pick up," Sam explained.

A waiter refilled champagne glasses, and the bidding began. I motioned with my glass. "One way to get people into the spirit."

The white-gloved assistant brought a painting onto the makeshift stage, and the auctioneer droned on about its provenance and worth. The oil had garish maroon and gold colors in various swirls and was more abstract than what I usually went for. I was in the minority because dozens of paddles lifted into the air as soon as he stopped speaking. The energy in the room was palpable, and if I had registered to bid, the crowd might have gotten me to go for a painting I didn't care for. The auctioneer slammed the gavel and said, "To bidder twenty-five for twenty thousand dollars.

I gasped and whispered to Rob. "Would you have gotten that?"

"They couldn't pay me to take it."

The next painting was of a little girl standing on a rickety dock staring wistfully out to sea. She had long brown hair in ringlets and wore a crisp white smock with a large baby blue bow. Paddles lifted, and the bidding was fierce.

"Cute, but she's never going to stay clean in that smock. A wave's surely going to hit her," I said.

"Sold for fifteen thousand dollars."

Sam leaned toward us. "I'm going to see if I can find where Becky wandered to."

"I think I've had enough." Rob asked me, "Want to stay?"

"Too rich for my blood. I wouldn't mind some air."

We walked up the stairs to the top deck. It hadn't been too bad in the lounge, but as we climbed higher, we could tell the ship was rocking. Rob said, "Are you sure she's out there? It's pretty windy."

Sam nodded. "Her favorite time. I think it's the artist in her."

There was a sign on the door, "Locked due to Weather."

"Guess she's not," I said.

"You don't know her—let's go to the pool deck." Sam pointed down one floor. The pool water sloshed over the sides, all the cushions had been removed from the chaises, and they had been stacked and chained to prevent movement.

I eyed the sea. "They're prepping for a blow. I hope it's not going to get worse than this."

We went down a floor, then walked under the covered passageway to the now-closed grill and the stairs that went up to the top deck. A chain was across them with another sign, "Top Deck Closed." Sam ducked under it and raced to the top.

"This isn't the best idea." Rob chased after her. "Sam, come back."

I waited a moment and then climbed after Rob. The swell was getting worse, and I had to hold onto both railings as I went. Sam and Rob were scanning the top deck. I pointed. "There."

Becky was on the other side of the ship, against one of the railings, and she climbed onto the lowest rung.

"What is she doing? Is she nuts?" Rob yelled due to the increasing wind.

"*Titanic* fetish. I wouldn't let her do it before." Sam began to run toward Becky, screaming for her to get down as we followed.

Rain began to pelt almost sideways, and waves climbed the ship with increasing fervor. Suddenly, a figure dressed in a dark rain slicker darted from a crew door, shoved Becky, and, without pausing, returned to the door, which slammed shut behind the person.

Sam screamed, "No," as Becky flew into the air and a white-capped wave lifted to meet her. Sam grabbed the ring buoy from its holder and flung it to the spot where Becky went into the water.

The loudspeaker boomed, "The crew drill is now over. Please return to your stations."

I saw several white-clad crew strolling across the pool deck and yelled, "Woman overboard."

They dashed up the stairs, one speaking a mile a minute into his walkie-talkie. Rob and Sam had kept their eyes and fingers pointed toward where Becky went in and where the ring buoy was now floating. An arm suddenly clutched it, and I could just make out Becky's head.

Rob shouted, "She has it."

As the cruise ship slowed to a crawl, I lost sight of Becky because the rolling waves were like a crazed washing machine on the spin cycle, spitting water everywhere. Rob, Sam, the crew, and I all lined the railing, trying to keep her in sight.

Sam pointed fifteen degrees south and west of where Becky had been. "There."

We were pulling further away, and Becky's head was smaller and smaller. It would have been almost impossible to see her had she not been clutching the white ring. The officer lifted the walkie-talkie and gave directions.

A roar was just audible over the ocean, and a rescue boat sped over the waves heading in Becky's direction. Sam was shaking, arm still outstretched as if she could grab Becky's hand and single-handedly pull her away from any danger. Her face was grim, and tears mixed with rain poured off her chin.

Rob hugged her. "It's okay. They'll get her. Thank goodness we saw where she went in."

"It's such a long fall." Sam's teeth chattered.

The ship lurched to a halt.

I rubbed Sam's back. "The wave was rising. It wasn't as bad as it could have been."

She pushed away from Rob. "Who did it? I'll kill him."

We could see the rescue boat again. And it was heading our way. "They must have her, or they'd still be searching."

"What if she didn't make it? What if the water was too cold? What if she got hypothermia?" She ran to the man with the walkie-talkie. "What did they say? Is she all right?"

"They have her. They're working on her now."

"What does that mean? Is she okay?"

Another officer strode toward us. "Chief Security Officer Patterson has some questions. Follow me."

"I'm going where that's going." Sam gestured toward the incoming boat.

"I have my instructions. You'll have to come with me." He crossed his arms.

Rob stepped forward. "That's her fiancée. How about we go with you, and you have someone take her to where the boat's coming in? Then, once Sam knows what's going on, I'm sure she'll answer any questions you have."

The man turned to one of the other officers. "Don't let her out of your sight. Bring her to the chief security officer's office once she's ready."

"They'll be coming in on deck five." The officer turned to Sam.

"What are we waiting for then? Let's go." Sam took off toward the stairs.

Chapter 16

Chief Security Officer Patterson shook his head. "I haven't had a cruise like this ever. Fights in restaurants, a bridge tour that had to be cut short, and now a woman overboard. And it's all the same family. Except for you two."

Rob and I sat in the officer's small, utilitarian office. The chairs weren't the plush ones we were used to from the public areas of the ship, though they had likely done that on purpose because if you were in the security office, you had crossed a line somewhere. Blankets shrouded our shoulders, and my rain-drenched hair was wrapped in a towel.

"I can explain," Rob said.

"I doubt it. You made us risk crew members' lives in a storm because you wanted to go out on deck. A deck that was clearly marked off-limits. Do you know how rough the seas are out there? Had you been drinking? Had she been drinking?"

"I had a glass of champagne, but—" Rob sputtered.

"You may be confined to your cabin for the rest of the cruise, and you may be barred from this line for life. This is serious."

He was making me madder by the moment, showing no sympathy for us in our wet clothes or poor Becky, who went overboard. I stood. "The officer suggested you had questions for us. I know what happened was bad, but if you don't let us answer, I think this is a waste of our time and yours."

"Why did you ignore the marked signs and chained stairs?" He fired off a question.

"Do you have a preference for who answers?" I asked.

He shook his head. I glanced at Rob, and he gestured I should take this one. I said, "We were at the art auction where we did have a glass of champagne. I didn't see Sam or Becky drink anything. Becky was not interested in the auction and said she was going to get fresh air." I paused. "Could I get a glass of water?"

He pressed a button on the phone, relayed the request, and then nodded for me to continue.

"We stayed to watch the bidding—it was fast and furious but way too expensive for us, so we decided to leave with Sam to find out where Becky had gone."

Rob broke in. "When we got to the top floor, the doors were locked, and a sign advised the deck was closed."

"And you decided to go out there anyway."

"We didn't see Becky if that was what you meant," I said.

He shrugged.

"Anyway, we went down to the pool deck. Sam was sure Becky was up on the top deck. Apparently, she's a *Titanic* fan. So, Sam ducked under the chain, and I followed," Rob explained. "I was worried about how rough it was and wanted to make sure Sam would be okay."

There was a sharp knock at the door, and a waiter brought in water for both of us. Rob took a long drink and continued. "We raced to the top deck—"

"I was behind Rob and went up because he chased after Sam, but when we got to the deck, I spotted Becky on the far side—"

"And then she climbed up one rung onto the railing," Rob said. "It was crazy—the ship's pitching, winds up, and she scales the rail. So stupid."

"What happened next?" The chief security officer asked.

"The scariest thing I've ever seen." I paused. "This guy runs out one of the crew doors straight for her. At first, I thought the guy was going to pull her off the railing to safety. But he didn't—he pushed her. And she went sailing into the sea. I can still see it when I shut my eyes." I shuddered.

"A man pushed her?" The officer asked.

"Don't know," Rob said. "Could have been a woman. From where I was standing, it seemed like whoever did it was about five foot eight to six feet tall."

"How did you know? Oh—you know how tall Becky is and that she was on the bottom rail." I nodded.

"And whoever did it was wearing a navy crew slicker," Rob added.

"What? How did you see that? I didn't notice..." I shook my head. "I just saw a black or navy slicker with a hood pulled over the person's head. How did I miss that?" I wondered aloud.

"Saw the lettering for a second as he turned to go back through the door."

"I must have been staring at Becky. It was so horrible. Thank goodness that wave came up. It would have been a huge drop if the sea had been calm." I groaned.

"So, you're accusing a crew member of pushing a guest overboard?" The officer scribbled on a pad.

Rob shook his head. "Didn't say that. Just as we don't know if it was a man or woman. The only thing I do know is that a jacket marked 'Crew' was worn, and the person came out of a 'Crew Only' door.

"At any rate, Sam tossed the life preserver after Becky, and I strained to keep sight of it and her. Merry yelled, 'Woman Overboard,' to the crew returning from the drill, and they took over from there. You should have seen how quickly Sam got the buoy out of its holder and over the rail. And that throw—perfection."

I grabbed Rob's arm. "When we were on the tour yesterday, there were all those monitors on the bridge. One of them must have been trained on that area of the deck." I turned to Chief Security Officer Patterson. "Don't you keep tapes of those? It should show what

146

happened. And there may have been a better angle as to who pushed her."

There was another sharp rap on the door, and a white-faced Sam walked in. I leaped to my feet and wrapped her in a hug. Are you okay? How's Becky?"

Rob pulled out the other chair, and I guided Sam to it. I turned to the chief security officer. "Can she get something hot? Tea or coffee? She's shaking."

He grumbled something about being an officer, not a waiter, but relayed the request.

Sam pulled the blanket she must have been given at the medical facility tighter around herself. "Becky's alive. The doctor said she swallowed a lot of seawater, broke her left wrist in the fall, and will have big bruises, but other than that, she's okay." She wiped tears from her face. "I wouldn't have been able to face life without her."

"Can he put a cast on? Or will that have to wait till we dock?" I asked.

"He can do it. He's keeping her under observation for now, but if all goes well, she can return to the room later tonight. He said she was lucky a wave broke her fall, or she might have faced a very different outcome."

A waiter brought a pot of tea and mug for Sam and poured it. She thanked him and lifted it to her lips, hand shaking. "Can't seem to get warm. They gave me coffee downstairs. Maybe after a long hot shower."

The chief security officer cleared his throat. "I have questions—"

"Would it be possible to let her shower and then do this later? You can see the state she's in." My chin jutted as I argued with him.

"We need to get to the bottom of this. Just a few questions, and then I will follow up with all of you later." He glanced at the pad in his hand. "I think I understand why you went up to the top deck... you were searching for your friend."

"My fiancée," Sam corrected.

"My apologies. What happened when you sighted her?"

Sam blew on the tea and sipped, cupping her hands around the mug. "I ran toward her. She had climbed onto the bottom rung. She tried to do it the other day, and I stopped her." She paused. "I should have let her. The skies were clear, and the ship wasn't rocking. Why didn't I let her do it? I thought we would look stupid—everyone on the deck sunning themselves. Why did I care?

"What was going through her mind today? It was so stupid. The rail was slick from ocean spray and rain. She could have slipped on her own—"

The chief security officer interrupted her musing, "Let's get back to the question, please. What did you see?"

"This guy came out the door nearest to her, crew slicker and all, and pushed her. I can't believe he pushed her. What kind of ship is this where you hire homicidal maniacs?"

"It was definitely a man?" Rob asked.

"Give me a moment." Sam stared at the wall. "Didn't see his face, but wouldn't it have to be? He pushed her. He pushed her off the ship." Sam began to cry again.

"Becky's going to be okay. She's going to be okay." I rubbed small circles on her back.

"I can't do this now." Sam swatted at the fat tears rolling down her face. "I just can't. I need a hot shower and sleep. I feel like I'm crashing."

"Adrenaline's wearing off," Rob said.

Chief Security Officer Patterson nodded. "Fine. But you are all confined to your rooms. I'll expect you back here at nine in the morning."

"But it's our last day. We were going to go ashore in the Bahamas..." I caught myself. "Never mind—momentary lapse. This is far more important."

"We'll take Sam back to her room and then go to ours. I'm exhausted too." Rob rose and helped Sam to her feet.

I joined them, and we left the depressing institutional gray corridors of the crew part of the ship for the vibrant public areas, attracting plenty of stares from people dressed in their finery for an early dinner due to our bedraggled hair and blanket-adorned clothes.

Dawn was on one of the glass-enclosed elevators, going up, and her hair was wet. I clutched Rob's hand and nodded toward it. His eyes widened.

We walked to the elevator bank and got on. Sam's suite was on the ninth floor too but on the other side of the boat. When we arrived at her door, I asked, "Are you going to be okay? Do you want me to come in with you?"

She seemed half asleep as she mumbled, "Going to phone the doctor for an update on Becky, take a shower, and fall into bed."

I gave her our room number and told her to call if she needed us. Then Rob and I walked to our suite. The steward was just leaving, and we handed him our used blankets and the towel from my head. He gave us an odd look but had obviously been trained not to ask questions.

Once we were inside and the door locked, I turned to Rob. "Did you see Dawn on the elevator?"

He nodded. "Suspicious. But it's been a while since Becky was pushed. Seems strange she'd still be wandering around on the ship like nothing had happened if she'd done it. Maybe she showered after a massage?

"Speaking of which, you want to shower first?"

I nodded, went into the bathroom, and shed my clothes. The hot water felt heavenly, but after only a few minutes of luxuriating, I felt guilty about making Rob wait for his, so I soaped, rinsed, and dried. I donned my robe and told Rob, "Your turn."

He kissed me on the nose. "I thought you were never coming out."

"Sorry." I walked into the closet and changed into shorts and a shirt. Then, I turned on the television and perused the room service menu. After a few moments, Rob joined me. "What are you doing?"

"Kind of hungry after all this action. Since we're confined to our room, I thought we'd see what was on the menu." I checked the clock. "We can order from the main restaurant or the room service menu. Says here they'll even serve us course by course."

"I don't want to see anyone more than we have to. Let's just order everything at once." As I scrolled, Rob said, "Go back a moment. I want the crab salad to start, and then a burger and fries. Plus, the chocolate mousse cake. Oh, and the biggest glass of wine they have."

I laughed. "Anything else?"

"It's been a very stressful day."

I picked up the phone and ordered.

The wind was howling even with the balcony door shut and locked. The room steward had brought in the outside cushions and placed them behind the closed drapes. I peeked out. "They've lashed our chairs to the balcony rail. I hope it's calmer tomorrow."

Rob gathered me into his arms. "I guess it's lucky we're confined to our suite. Might be dangerous walking in the hallways."

"It seems like it's treacherous just being on the ship." I plopped onto the sofa and patted the seat next to me. Rob sat, and I continued, "Correct me if you think I'm wrong, but it would be a wild coincidence if a crew member tried to kill Becky after Butch was killed, Dawn got sick, and Randy's zip line broke or was cut."

"I agree with your assessment." Rob put his arm around my shoulders.

"So, how did it happen? How could anyone know Becky would be on the top deck in rough seas? And how did they know where the crew door led to?"

"Strikes me that it had to be someone who knew Becky well. Someone who knew about the *Titanic* thing. And as to how they would know where the crew door went, maybe they didn't. They could have ducked in there to wait and then gone back after pushing her. After you sounded the alarm, there was a lot of crew on deck, and many had on the same slicker. He or she could easily have slipped away." Rob stretched his legs onto the coffee table.

"That's taking a chance. What if someone had come across him or her?"

"Don't forget—the crew drill was going on. So, he or she would have been able to blend in and make their escape." The doorbell rang, and Rob went to get it.

The waiter laid a white cloth over our table and made perfect settings for knives, forks, spoons, and crisp napkins. Then she deposited the various dishes we had requested, and finally, she produced two wine glasses and a large carafe of red wine.

Rob thanked her and escorted her to the door. When he returned, I took the desk chair, moved it to the table, and gestured for him to take the sofa. Then, I took the silver lids off the plates, inhaled the peppery smell of basil from my fusilli pasta, and said, "I'm so hungry. I didn't think I'd be able to eat after everything that happened, but now, I'm afraid I didn't order enough."

"I guess it's a good thing I ordered a lot then." Rob lifted a fork ladened with crab.

I poured us both wine and then sprinkled grated parmesan on my meal. Mushrooms, red peppers, and sausage were nestled amongst the pasta, and I took a large bite. I covered my mouth with my napkin and mumbled, "I'm afraid there's a lot of garlic. You may not want to get too close to me tonight."

He leaned across the table and kissed me. "One can't ever have too much garlic. Plus, I expect you to let me have a little in exchange for a bit of my crab?"

I slid a small portion onto my bread plate and handed it over. He followed suit.

"This is luscious...and the capers. Yum."

"Not to interfere with our digestion, but if we agree it was a stretch that it was a crew member, who could it have been?" Rob took a bite of the pasta. "This is good."

"You're sure about the five foot eight-six footish? And are you sure it could have been a woman? Wouldn't it be hard to get that kind of leverage on Becky?"

"On both questions, yes. It would have been much harder if Becky had been on the deck. Think of it like a fulcrum." Rob lifted his right arm and bent it." She was on the bottom rung, which meant her waist was above the top rail. It wouldn't take a hard shove to unbalance her and send her over." He hit his hand with his other fist, and his right arm was pushed down. "See?"

I nodded as I lifted bread from the basket. "I have to shut my eyes every time I think about it... Her flying through the air. I'm so glad all she ended up with was a broken wrist."

"She was lucky." Rob sipped wine and then cut his cheddar cheeseburger in half. "Want some?"

"Maybe a quarter."

He cut it again and handed it to me. "Who does that leave us?"

"Michael, Dawn, Sheila, and Randy. They're all about that height."

"Doesn't narrow it down much. It's a good thing Sam was with us, or she might be a suspect." I put ketchup on a plate and dipped a fry in it. "The person didn't seem that big to me. Randy's girth would give him away. Plus, he was still limping the last time I saw him. But I didn't see the writing on the jacket, so perhaps my perception isn't to be relied upon."

Rob shook his head. "Different angle than Sam and me, not that you missed something. And I have to agree with you. I don't think it was Randy."

"So now we need to find out where people were later this afternoon and if anyone can vouch for them. I can only hope they got whoever it was on the recording."

"You think the security guy will tell us?"
"We can only ask."

Chapter 17

Rob read the Cruise Line's newsletter while I brushed my teeth. I wandered out of the bathroom and mumbled, "Do they mention anything about Becky going overboard?"

"Not something they'd advertise. Especially if they think one of their guys did it."

"But lots of people saw us when we came out of the crew area. Wouldn't they have questions?"

"They didn't see her go overboard—the top deck was closed, remember?"

I walked back to the bathroom, rinsed, and then said, "How could I forget? I hope we can get out of this cabin sometime today. I guess the good news is we'll have plenty of time to pack."

"Will you be happy to go home?" Rob put the newsletter to the side as I walked into the room.

"I can't wait to see Jenny again, though I hate to think what Drew's been up to. I'll feel better leaving if we can figure out what's happening here."

"Agreed. You ready for some more questions?"

"I guess." I walked to the balcony and opened the drapes. The sky was a brilliant blue without a single cloud, and the sea had left its steel gray behind and gone back to the turquoise for which the Caribbean is known. A white sand beach next to the pier beckoned.

I opened the door to a slight breeze and walked outside, where it was warm and a calypso band played under a palapa across the street.

Colorful shirts and wraps hung from the thatched roofs of the open-air shops.

I sighed. "I wanted to get Jenny one last gift."

Rob laughed. "I don't think we can fit everything in our suitcases as it is." He joined me on the balcony and wrapped his arms around me. "Maybe we can get out of house arrest and wander around in town."

"I don't want to get my hopes up." Streams of passengers exited the boat and headed out on tours. "I guess we should go—wouldn't want to be late."

Rob locked the balcony door, and we left. As we walked to the security office, I said, "I'm going to miss the pampering, but I can't wait to get back to my house to try new recipes."

"Our house." Rob lifted my hand and kissed it.

"Our house." I smiled.

The door to the office was open, so I stood in it and asked the chief security officer, "Ready for us?"

He waved us in. "Good morning."

Four chairs were arrayed in front of his desk—Rob and I sat in the two on the left.

"Give me a minute." Just as he finished typing, there was a rap on the door. Sam and Becky hesitated on the threshold. Her left wrist was in a cast from her palm and thumb to just below her elbow. As she came in, she walked slowly and with a slight limp. When Sam put her hand on Becky's other arm, she winced.

Rob and I got to our feet. "Are you okay...How do you feel...We were so worried." We talked over each other.

She raised her right hand. "I'm fine. Except for my stupid wrist. I still can't believe what happened."

Sam guided her into a chair, then held onto her hand like he never wanted to let Becky go again.

Becky sat. "I'm fine. Stop fussing."

"As I told you, I could have come to your cabin if you had been more comfortable there," the chief security officer said.

"Let's get this over with." Becky sat back in the chair.

"What did you find on the security tapes?" I leaned forward.

"We'll get to that." He turned to Becky. "Can you tell me what you saw?"

"The ocean rushing toward me at what seemed like a hundred miles an hour. It felt like I hit concrete when I landed. The doc told me if it had been a calm day, I would never have made it."

"Did you see who pushed you?"

"I was facing the sea, dreaming I was on the ship's bow. A proud Valkyrie leading us forward into the unknown, mists gathering, and new worlds to explore." She frowned. "It would have been better if I had been on the bow. Speaking of which—why is that part of the ship off-limits? Only crew can get out there. I was thinking about my next series of paintings. Angry dark blues, white froth—"

"Ms. Calhoun, if we could get back to the subject..." Officer Patterson said.

"Sorry. Sometimes I get carried away—where was I? Oh, yes—no—I did not see who pushed me."

"Why did you climb onto the railing?"

"Sam said they already told you." She turned a bright shade of pink.

"I'd like to hear it from you."

"I'm a romantic. I love that scene and have done it on every ship we've been on. This, however, is the only ship on which I've been thrown overboard."

He said, "We're investigating that. Didn't the other ships object to you climbing the rails?"

Becky shrugged. "Some. It hasn't been a big deal till here."

"But you could have fallen. And you did fall this time."

"Believe me—I won't be doing it again." She raised her casted arm.

Rob said, "I think you've gotten all you're going to be able to get from us. A crime has been committed—what are you doing about it?"

"I'm asking the questions." He had the good grace to shift in his chair and seem a little discomforted. "All right, let's play the video. We're questioning the crew—maybe you'll recognize the person."

He turned the flat screen toward us and pressed play on his laptop. The footage was grainy, and the previous day's pelting rain didn't help as water dripped from the camera. It showed Becky climbing onto the rail and then the person pushing her. He or she was clearly wearing a crew slicker, as the angle was from the rear. When the person turned to run back to the door, his or her head was ducked, and the slicker was pulled low, making it impossible to discern any features. The chief security officer pressed pause. "Look like anyone you've seen around the ship?"

We leaned closer to the monitor.

"There's something…" I tapped my fingers on the desk. "Not coming to me. Could you run it back again?"

I pulled my chair closer to the desk and studied the footage as it replayed. "Stop for a moment."

He paused the recording.

"No. Nothing."

He hit play.

It trailed to the end. I shook my head. "Not coming to me. I don't know what I thought I saw. But it was something—I'm going to have to think about it."

Rob stood. "Anything else?"

"One more thing." Officer Patterson turned to Becky and Sam. "You are confined to your room until we dock tomorrow morning."

Sam shrugged. "Thought that was coming. Becky's not well enough to be doing much anyway. Guess I'll just pack."

I crossed my fingers.

"Ms. March and Mr. Jenson—you are free to move about the ship and go ashore, but please, no more trouble."

A smile lighted Rob's lips. "Great—one last day of exploring. I assure you—we'll be as good as clergy."

I worried he was over-promising.

Chapter 18

After making sure Sam could handle getting Becky back to the cabin, Rob and I practically ran back to ours. I changed into shorts and a shirt and slathered sunscreen. Then I grabbed a hat, sunglasses, and bag. "Ready?"

Rob chuckled. "I was born ready. Why do I feel like we're kids escaping from the principal on the last day of school."

"Maybe because we are." I slipped my hand through his, and we made our way off the ship to the shopping plaza beyond.

"I think this area concentrates on cruise ships," Rob said as we passed another store whose large sign proclaimed 'Duty Free.'"

I stopped in front of a jewelry store window, captivated by a gossamer silver necklace, almost like a spider had spent weeks weaving it.

Rob pointed. "Want it?"

"Too expensive. After the trip and the wedding, I should focus on getting Jenny or someone else something."

"Mac and Mother paid for the trip as a wedding gift—we can treat ourselves." He pushed me gently toward the door. "You'll regret not getting it. Let's at least go in."

I laughed. "Okay, but if I don't absolutely love it, I'm not going to buy it."

"Deal."

The store was crowded with last-minute cruise shoppers, so it took a few minutes for someone to assist us. She removed the necklace from the case, and Rob fastened it around my neck. I lifted the mirror—the silver shone on my skin, twinkling in the shop light as I turned right and left. I turned to Rob, "Are you sure?"

"Yes." He smiled.

Still undecided, I moved the mirror to see different angles as my fingers traced the filigree. It was simple, three chains of different lengths that flowed and became one near the back, but the silver's shine and craftsmanship were stunning. It was an indulgence, but I deserved it. I was about to hand the mirror back to the saleswoman when I noticed Sheila and Randy on the other side of the store. Sheila was holding a ring, and Randy was shaking his head. She seemed upset.

Rob asked, "Can I buy it for you?"

"Behind you, to your left," I whispered.

He turned. "That's not going to end well."

"Do you think we could get closer to hear what they're saying?" I handed the necklace back to the saleswoman. "We're going to take this, but we want to browse a bit first.

"Let's look at earrings for Jenny. I think there are cute ones over there." I moved closer to Randy and Sheila, keeping my head down.

Rob followed, and we examined the earrings. I said, "These are cute."

Randy grumbled, "You can't get that ring. We're going to have to tighten our belts for a while till everything gets resolved."

"If you loved me, you'd buy it." She pouted. "It's the perfect brown to match my eyes. A champagne diamond—I've always wanted one."

"You have a dozen cocktail rings. You don't need another."

"One can never have too much of anything. We have plenty of money. Why are we scrimping now?"

"Because Dawn has me over a barrel. She could charge me with assault." He shook his head. "This is serious—I may be out of a job when I get back."

"I wasn't the idiot who confessed in front of an entire audience."

"You told me to do it." His face began to turn red.

"Don't turn this on me. You could have told me no." She turned to the salesperson. "I'm getting this."

"You are not getting it." Randy's voice rose.

Their salesperson asked, "Would you like me to ring it up?"

"No."

"Yes."

"You should have kept your job instead of relying on me. Do you know how much stress I'm under while you play with your bits and bytes?" Randy roared.

"Fine. I don't want it." Sheila slammed the ring onto the counter, turned on her heel, and marched from the store.

Randy stared after her, teeth grinding. After a moment, he turned to the salesperson. "I'd better get it. Quick, before I change my mind." He thrust a credit card toward her.

Most everyone in the store had turned to watch the spectacle—now that it was over, they resumed their browsing. Rob asked, "Ready to go?"

I pointed to a pair of plain gold hoops. "Let's get these for Jenny."

He told the saleswoman, "These too."

As she was charging Rob's card, Randy stalked from the store. I nudged Rob. "There's trouble in paradise."

"I wonder how Sheila's going to adapt to having her purchases restricted."

"If that was any indication—not well. Of course, he did acquiesce in the end."

Rob took the bag from the saleswoman, thanked her, and we exited the store. "More shopping?" he asked.

"It'll just tempt me."

Seagrape trees lined the avenue, shading the benches underneath, and a wide swath of blindingly white sand lay between them and the ocean. Our ship stood proudly at the pier but was mostly ignored by the people walking past on the sidewalk. Vendors with colorful carts lined the street, and I made a beeline for one advertising fresh squeezed lemonade. "Want one?" I asked Rob.

He nodded.

I told the man two and pointed toward an empty bench. "Rob, why don't you grab that one, and we'll people watch."

He obliged while I waited for the man to squeeze the fruit and add sugar and water. He took two plastic cups, scooped shaved ice, and then added the lemonade, presenting them with a flourish. I thanked him and joined Rob.

"This is yummy and just what I needed. Thank you," Rob said as he slurped.

People played frisbee on the beach while others manned barbecues from which the tantalizing smells of grilled chicken emerged. Children splashed in the cerulean sea, and a volleyball net was in the process of being staked.

"Seems hard to believe tomorrow we'll be on our way home to the cold," I mused.

"Back to reality. But before long, it'll be Christmas, and you know how much you love decorating for the season." Rob draped his arm behind me on the bench.

"I do. And this year will be even more special because you'll be there."

"Don't forget. Mother and Mac are planning a big 'do' on Christmas Eve," Rob said.

"Way to ruin a mood."

He chuckled. "She's trying to be less controlling and judgmental."

"I know, and she has gotten better. Plus, they were so gracious to give us this trip. I'm sure it will be a delightful time."

"Don't get carried away." Rob nudged me.

A man emerged from the water and turned to give his companion a lengthy kiss with nary an inch separating their bodies. The woman laughed and ran to the shore, dropping onto a large white towel with the cruise ship's logo prominently displayed. My mouth formed a perfect oval, and Rob asked, "What's up?"

"That's Dawn and Michael."

"So?"

"Unless he were performing standing mouth-to-mouth, I'd say they are definitely an item. The question is how long it's been going on."

"Want to wander over there and see what we can find out?"

I nodded, grabbed Rob's empty cup, paired it with mine, and threw it in the trash. "Let's go."

The couple was lying close together on the towels, and Michael nuzzled Dawn's neck. Her eyes widened as we approached. She pushed him away, rose to her feet, and brushed sand from her legs. Michael turned toward us and scowled.

"Couldn't help but notice you. It's nice to have a last day off the ship, isn't it?" I said.

"It was until we were interrupted." Michael stood as well.

"You seemed pretty friendly," Rob quipped.

"Not your business." Dawn's arms were crossed, and her lips taut.

"True. But we couldn't help but wonder when this fondness for each other started. Was it before your husband left this world?"

"I loved my husband," Dawn insisted.

"Uh-huh," I said.

The two sides had arrived to play volleyball, and the scrimmage on either side was raucous. Rob stepped closer to Michael. "The attorney and the wife?"

Michael took a swing at him, and Rob ducked.

"Stop it!" Dawn yelled.

Michael took a step back, breathing heavily, eyes flat and black. "None of your business, Rob."

"I know how this must seem, but you have to believe me. All these late hours, pouring over documents, getting everything set for the board meeting in New York—we grew close. Nothing happened until the last few days." She clasped Michael's hand. "It's been tough. But Michael made it easier. I needed someone who was on my side."

"Heard enough?" Michael spat.

Rob held up his hands. "Hey, just seemed a little suspicious to my questioning nature, and I know Dawn wants everything to go smoothly in front of the board."

"Is that a threat?" Dawn's face colored, and Michael took another step toward Rob.

"Don't be silly," I said. "Rob was just stating a fact."

"I think I've had enough sun for one day." Dawn yanked her towel away from the sand, shook it so most of what was on it landed on Rob and me, and stalked toward the ship.

Michael hesitated, glaring at Rob.

She turned, "Michael, let's go."

"I don't forgive, and I don't forget," Michael growled, then ran after Dawn.

"That was kind of scary." I wandered back to the bench we had been sitting on.

"You weren't the one he wanted to flatten." Rob sat next to me.

"Was it wise to get him riled up?" I asked.

"Running out of time—we have to try to shake things loose."

"We seemed so mean. Especially if they had nothing to do with Butch's death." I shivered.

Rob glanced at his watch. "We should start packing. Plus, the chicken smell is making me hungry. Want to go back?"

"I guess. To tell the truth, I'm a little hungry too."

164

We joined the queue of people waiting to get on the ship. Some were juggling large packages, which made me wonder if they had brought a spare suitcase with them for the express purpose of housing their purchases. I laughed. "Sheila probably brought six extra suitcases for all of her loot."

"What do you think is going on with her and Michael?" Rob inched forward in line.

"He's moved to greener pastures or at least one with better prospects."

"How does Sheila feel about that?" His eyebrow rose.

"And does she know things between Dawn and Michael have progressed that far?"

We handed our key cards to the security staff person at the bottom of the gangplank, and when we got to the top, Rob put our stuff onto the conveyor belt to be sent through the metal detector. Then, Rob posed for the facial recognition camera, and I followed. Sufficiently declared to be who we were and that we had no contraband, we boarded the ship and ran up the stairs to the room.

As Rob inserted the key card, he turned to me. "Why do I think you're going to cause even more trouble?

"You started it, dear husband." I kissed him on the cheek and ducked past him into the room.

Chapter 19

We decided on the more relaxed pool grill for lunch, and Rob was lucky because they had barbecued chicken. I ordered iced tea and Rob a beer. While he people-watched, I perused the menu, landing on a spicy tuna poke bowl. After we ordered, Rob said, "That seems pretty healthy for the last day."

"Couldn't help myself—it sounds so fresh and light. Plus, that way, I don't have to feel guilty when I indulge in an ice cream cone afterward." I sipped tea as I spied Randy and Sheila scanning the restaurant for a table. I half stood and waved. "Join us."

Sheila turned toward Randy—he shrugged, and they came to the table and sat. "Thanks. It's a little crowded today."

The waiter took their order.

"What a beautiful ring," I exclaimed. "Is it new?"

"Just this morning." Sheila patted Randy's hand. "Wonderful husband."

Her nails were a deep blue and evenly shaped. Mine had been done before the wedding, but nearly two weeks later were in dire need of freshening up. *Nails.* My eyes widened. That's what I had seen—just a flash on the tape. The person who pushed Becky wore nail polish. It wasn't blue, though, it was a rose-red, from what I remembered. I was going to have to get the chief security officer to show me the video again.

Conversation at the table had ceased, and everyone was staring at me. I said, "Sorry, wool gathering—was there a question?"

"Were you able to get off the ship this morning? Becky said she and Sam were confined to quarters."

"We were lucky. They decided since we had gone upstairs fearing for Sam and Becky's safety, one night's confinement was punishment enough. Had room service and, to tell the truth, it was nice to have downtime. Especially after seeing Becky go overboard—one of the scariest things ever." I shuddered. "Needed two glasses of wine."

"I can't believe how stupid she was," Randy said. "Sometimes that girl—" He stopped himself. "I'm glad she's safe, and the only thing broken was her wrist."

"She isn't known for her brains." Sheila shook her head.

"Artistic." Randy shrugged. "But a good sister overall."

"She was talking about the investments she's made at dinner with the captain the other night. She seemed pretty sharp—like she knew what she was doing," Rob interjected. "And Dawn seemed impressed by her knowledge."

"Like Dawn knows everything." Randy rolled his eyes.

"Speaking of which, Dawn and Michael were getting pretty close on the beach this morning. I think they're going to be a couple," I said.

The color on Sheila's face rose as food was delivered to the table. It almost rivaled Rob's barbecue sauce. "What are you talking about?" she sputtered.

"They seemed quite chummy, and that lip lock..." Rob fanned his face. "Not one to tell tales, but things must be moving quickly."

"I knew it." Randy threw his napkin to the table. "She's been planning this all along. She was never in love with my father."

The waiter nervously approached. "I'm sorry, sir, but I'm going to have to ask you to keep it down. The guests—"

"I'm tired of you people telling me what to do." He stood. "First, you let my father die, then my sister's thrown overboard, and now that witch of a wife of his is going to get away with murder."

There was an audible gasp at some of the other tables because he spoke quite loudly.

The chief security officer strode to our table. "Mr. Calhoun, I'm going to have to ask you to leave. And since you continue to cause disturbances in our restaurants and the theater, you will be required to stay in your cabin until we dock tomorrow. Please, accompany me."

Randy sputtered as the chief security officer led him away.

"Well, thank heavens he's gone." Sheila leaned forward. "What exactly did you see between Michael and Dawn?"

I told her. When I finished, she stood and strode from the table without saying another word.

"Well, that was interesting, but now my chicken's cold," Rob complained.

"Luckily, mine was cold to begin with." I smirked as I took a bite.

"Good barbecue is worth eating either way. But I need new fries." He beckoned the waiter, who soon returned with them.

I snagged one from his plate and almost dropped it. "Hot."

"Just the way I like them." Rob lifted one and then paused. "Merry, with all the pot stirring we've been doing, we're going to have to be very careful for one more day."

Officer Patterson plopped into the chair Randy had vacated, and a waiter hurriedly removed the uneaten food, set a new place, and brought him coffee. He said, "Trouble seems to follow you both."

"I remembered something," I lifted another of Rob's fries. "But to be certain, I'll need to see the video again."

He stood. "Let's go. I'll eat later."

"But we're not finished," Rob muttered, spearing a piece of chicken.

"I'm ready. I can come back later for dessert." I rubbed Rob's shoulder. "No time like the present."

We got up and followed the chief security officer to his office, where he turned on his laptop and played the video. We watched it again, and even though the video wasn't the best quality, now that I knew what I was searching for, it was easier. "Stop and zoom in."

He paused it, and I pointed to the blurry perpetrator's hand. As Becky went overboard, there was a flash of red. "Do it in slow motion."

He obliged and said, "Son of a Gun. That nail is painted red."

"Sure is. Now we know we're looking for someone with painted nails. And that someone is most likely a woman. The only question is which one."

* * *

Rob put the suitcases on top of the goodbye mat the steward had left on the bed for that purpose. I ferried our clothes from the closet into the bedroom, and Rob levered them into the bag. He said, "It makes it much easier to pack when your clothes are already clean."

"Love the fact that they do your laundry for you. Will make going home much easier—just have to put it into drawers. And you'll be happy to know I have a few empty ones waiting for you."

He kissed my cheek. "Thanks. A few?"

"Take what you can get." I grinned as I walked back into the closet. "Want to double-check we each have an outfit for the plane home tomorrow. A friend told me a cruise story where she saw a pair of jeans hanging on a hook and thought they were hers, and her husband thought they were his. She was quite unhappy to discover all of her pants were packed, and she would be touring Alaska in her nightgown."

"I thought once the bags left your room, you wouldn't see them again till customs."

"The front desk guy took pity on them, and her husband had to go into the bowels of the ship to identify their bags from amongst the thousands stacked high and ready to be unloaded. Good thing they had distinctive bands around them."

Rob nodded as he tucked the last of the socks between the clothes and the walls of the suitcase. "Anything else?"

"Just the stuff in the bathroom. We'll do that after dinner—they don't have to be out in the hall until eleven."

"One done, one to go." He zipped the full bag and placed it on the floor at the end of the desk near the door.

I lifted it and groaned. "Feels heavier than when we came. Hopefully, we won't exceed the airline's weight limit."

"Now what?"

"Java. I feel the need."

We jogged down to the coffee shop and perused the menu. "I missed out on ice cream—I'm getting the caramel macchiato."

"Iced coffee, cream, honey, for me," Rob told the barista and then walked to the food stations. One displayed all of the things you would find on an upscale charcuterie board—prosciutto, parma ham, assorted cheeses, and fruit, and the other, dainty pastries.

The tables outside were deserted, so when I retrieved our coffees, one of the servers opened the door, and I wandered outside to the farthest bistro table and put them down. Then, I joined Rob, who was in the process of piling various meats and cheeses onto a tiny plate. "Maybe you should see if they could get you a larger one," I quipped.

"Very funny. I left half my lunch on the plate. Then you had me packing for hours."

I tapped my watch. "An exaggeration if ever I heard one. Besides, you do it so much better than me—all those trips." I took a plate and added a tiny millefeuille and madeleine.

"When I was traveling for work, I traveled light."

"Are you complaining?" We made our way to the table.

"Never." He put his plate down, sat, and dove in.

I lifted my cup, and the scent of caramel and vanilla grew stronger. My eyes closed as I savored the taste. Then I lifted my fork and tried the millefeuille. "Heaven. Why have we never tried this buffet?"

"Busy," Rob mumbled as he downed a last piece of ham. Then he layered a slice of prosciutto onto a cracker with a tiny amount of brie. "I'm going to miss this."

"Should we go into town again? We have another few hours before we leave the island."

"I'm good." He took another bite of a cheese-laden cracker.

"Uh oh." Sheila was steaming toward Dawn, who was ordering a coffee at the bar inside.

"What?" Rob turned.

"This should be interesting. Too bad we can't listen in."

Their conversation seemed heated, and the waiter gestured for them to take it outside. I smiled. "We may have a ringside seat after all."

They stormed out the door. Sheila was mid-stride. "They've confined Randy to quarters, and it's all your fault, you slut."

"I don't know what you're talking about." Dawn sniffed, cool as a day in January.

"Why don't you ask them?" Sheila pointed to our table.

"Uh oh. They're coming this way," I told Rob, who had his back to them.

He rose. "Ladies, I'm not sure what this is all about, but—"

"You told me you caught this one and Michael 'in flagrante delicto,'" Sheila stated.

"We weren't copulating—we were kissing, you idiot. Not that it's any of your business." Dawn leaned against the rail and examined her French-tipped nails. "Why would you even care if Michael and I are growing closer—it's not like you're dating him—you're married to Randy."

Sheila's face flushed, and she stuttered, "Because...because... what about Butch?"

"He's dead. I'm not, and if I want to have a little fun, I should be allowed." Dawn walked toward the door. "I'm done here."

"No, you're not." Sheila grabbed her arm. "We're going to have this out."

Michael opened the door. "Been looking everywhere for you, darling."

Both Dawn and Sheila turned toward him, and Dawn shoved Sheila's hand from her arm and hissed, "Too bad you weren't the one who went overboard." Dawn threaded her hand between Michael's arm and chest and said, "Sorry, let's get our coffee and go. It's a bit crowded out here."

I thought I was going to need a vise to shut my mouth. Had Dawn really just said that?

Rob walked toward Sheila, "Are you okay?"

She glared at him and stalked out the door.

"Oh my." I put the madeleine in my mouth.

"What did that last bit mean? Did Dawn pitch Becky from the ship? Was that a confession?" Rob asked.

"Her nails weren't the right color. But we did see her going up in the elevator after Becky was pushed, and her hair was wet."

"By my tally, we're down to two suspects, Dawn and Sheila. Sheila's nails were blue, and Dawn's were clear with white tips. So, who pushed Becky?" Rob finished his last cracker.

"I think I might want to get my nails freshened before we dock tomorrow. Want to come with me to see if I can get an appointment?"

Rob nodded.

We traveled to the spa at the other end of the ship.

Chapter 20

The spa was relatively empty—our fellow travelers were most likely using the last afternoon of the cruise for shopping, packing, or eating. I checked in with the attendant and then wandered to the nail polish display—they must have been getting ready for the next onslaught of passengers because I had the complete and orderly array of colors to peruse. Focusing on the reds, I picked two, plus a deep royal purple and the blue I was sure Sheila had been wearing at lunch and made my way to the technician.

"I'm having a hard time deciding." I handed her the ones I had selected and then continued, "You must be getting quite a few customers for touch-ups before they go home."

She took the bottles from me and put them in a line. "Actually, the beginning of the cruise is far busier because everyone wants to look their best. By the end, people are rushing, trying to do everything they meant to but didn't. That plus packing." She paused. "You have quite a variety. These reds are always popular. And purple is a great choice, especially if you are going back to winter." Then she touched the top of the blue one. "I did this for someone just this morning. Odd—usually that's such a summer color—people only get it at the beginning of a cruise or when someone cruises back-to-back."

I leaned forward. "I saw someone with a fresh manicure earlier, and I think it was this color. She was tall, curvy, and had long brown hair."

"That's her. Did you like the job I did?" the technician asked.

"Wonderful. Do you remember what color she was taking off?"

She shrugged. "She must have had it done before she got on the ship—it wasn't one of ours. Might have been red or pink. To be honest, I don't remember. Is it important?"

"Just curious. I'll go with purple."

We chit-chatted as she worked, and as soon as she was done, I met Rob on the top deck. "Sounds like it was Sheila—the woman said someone who looked like her did a color change this morning. Maybe she knew we saw her and decided to get them done."

He shifted his feet so I could sit at the end of the chaise in the shade and said, "I doubt it. More likely, in the struggle, her nail was torn. Did the technician say anything about any repairs?"

"I didn't ask, darn it. Uh oh."

"What's wrong?"

I pointed to an expensive storefront on the island called "Tranquility." The door was heavy mahogany, and the walls were a muted dusky pink. A fountain with blue and white delft tiles dominated a private plant-laden courtyard we could see from the top of the ship.

"So?" He turned.

"Very upscale spa chain I read about with locations in Venice, New York, Los Angeles, and apparently here. I've always wanted to go, but it's so expensive it's hard to justify. Plus, I'm not a jet setter. I'm surprised Sheila didn't go there."

"Maybe you need an appointment."

"Not the issue—what if Dawn went there?"

"I think we're going to have to go off the ship again."

I nodded.

* * *

We stood in front of the forbidding door, and Rob said, "Let me make sure I have this right. My girlfriend is Dawn Franklin, and she thinks she left her phone at her appointment today."

"Go for it. I'll wait here."

I took a seat on a bench near the shop and watched the masked boobies dive bombing the fish in the harbor. Several locals on a pier had their rods out—they and the birds were vying for the same prey, and the street vendors were doing a brisk business as tour groups returned with cruisers eager for that one last deal before going home.

I glanced at the spa door. Would Dawn have pushed Becky overboard? It certainly seemed like she had threatened Sheila. Maybe Dawn did have it in her. But how would she benefit? My brow furrowed. That was a puzzler. Dawn was already going to inherit the lion's share of Butch's estate. I couldn't see it, unless Dawn would somehow benefit from Becky's death for an odd reason.

"Ready?"

I jumped. "Sorry. Lost in my thoughts. What did they say?"

The ship's horn blew, and Rob said, "Better hustle. Don't want to be one of those people they video running down the pier as the ship leaves."

"They wouldn't go without us, would they?"

"You bet. Let's move it."

We hustled up the gangplank and went to our room. As Rob scanned the keycard, another horn blew, and the ship began to move. I said, "That was closer than I would have liked."

Then, I sank onto the sofa, fanning myself with my hat. "Don't keep me in suspense. Tell me what you found out."

"She was there this morning to have her nails done. I insisted on speaking with the nail technician, even though they told me anything left behind would have been brought to the front desk. When she arrived, I told her that, although I liked the new nails, I preferred the old color better. And she said, 'Tempestuous Red?'"

I groaned. "So, it still could have been either one of them."

"You got it."

I stood. "Think anyone's in the library?"

"Probably people returning books. Speaking of which—" He motioned to the stack next to the bed.

"The return table is in the front. What I was asking is do you think anyone will be in the back, by the computers?"

"Let's find out." Rob scooped up several books, and I took the remainder.

"I haven't finished this one. I hate to leave one-half read." I muttered.

"Going to finish it tonight?"

"Nope."

Rob opened the door for me to go through. "I'll buy it for you at the airport."

We traveled to the eleventh floor, and I glanced through the door to the pool. "There are still people out there."

"Last rays before winter."

I sighed, and we walked toward the library. Someone exiting held the door, and we thanked her as we went past and put the books on the crowded return table. As predicted, all the action was near the door, and the computers were empty. I sat, and Rob dragged a chair next to me.

"What are we looking for?" Rob asked.

"Sheila. It seems like we've investigated everyone but her." I pulled up a search engine and typed her name. Dozens of photos came back of her at various charity functions, always quite glamorous, dripping with jewels. One of the society pages covered her and Randy's wedding and mentioned her maiden name. I tried that next.

"Computer Wunderkind Develops Artificial Intelligence Breakthrough" was the heading of one story with a picture of Sheila at about the age of the one with her and Michael at the prom—her proud parents stood on either side of her and beamed at the camera. The backdrop for the picture was dramatic—a cliff with the ocean as its backdrop, waves crashing.

"That's a beautiful place. I wonder where this picture was taken—it's familiar for some reason." I tried to recall where or when I had seen it before, but nothing came to me. I shrugged and scrolled further. "Science and Technology Movers and Shakers" was another headline. I went through the articles, with Rob reading over my shoulder, and then he sat back.

Rob said, "She's some kind of computer savant."

"Why would she have given that up to be a society person?" I read a few more articles and accolades. "I don't understand all the jargon, but it seems she was sought after for her expertise."

Then there was a more recent piece detailing how an unnamed corporation had hired her to solidify their systems against hackers. "She hadn't quite hung up her laptop." I sat back. "Wait a minute—something puzzled me this morning when Randy and Sheila were arguing. I thought he said bits and bites, which seemed strange. He actually said, 'bits and bytes.' He was talking about her dabbling with computers."

Rob and I turned toward each other and, in unison, said, "The snake."

Chapter 21

I asked, "But how could she have done it? She wasn't even there. Could she have hacked into the computer's system remotely?"

"I would think infiltrating the computer's games would be pretty easy for a person of her caliber. If she's helping companies fend off attackers, she'd have to be familiar with the weaknesses of various systems."

"And she'd have known Butch had a bad heart." I gasped. "That's terrible. She killed her father-in-law. I don't understand it—I'm sure companies pay big money for people with her skills. She could have made it on her own—she didn't need his money."

"Who knows why people do the things they do? But Sheila would also have to know how to do computer animation. Believe me, that snake was realistic—if I had a bad ticker, it would have knocked me down too." Rob absently rubbed his chest.

I continued to scroll. "She wouldn't necessarily need to know how to do it herself. It's not a big leap to assume she has computer-savvy friends, especially with the work she's done in artificial intelligence."

"Now what? We know for sure there was a snake—I saw it, but no one else did, and as far as the ship is concerned, Butch died of a heart attack. But we do have Dawn's mishap on the raft."

"Don't forget Randy poisoning Dawn—maybe he and his wife were in it together?" I paused. "Wait a minute. We also have Randy's fall on the zip line. Why would he have been in danger if he was in it with her?"

"And would he have wanted Becky to die?"

"All great questions and, except for Becky going overboard, which was seen by us and the camera, we don't have proof any of it happened the way we think it did." Rob frowned.

"Let's go back to our room and write it all down. Then our next step is to find Chief Security Officer Patterson and put it in front of him. We dock tomorrow, and we can't let her get away with this."

* * *

The chief security officer's chair squealed as he leaned back. "You make a compelling case, but I'm not hearing you have any proof. The only verifiable thing is that the person who pushed Ms. Becky Calhoun overboard had a painted fingernail. And that fingernail could belong to Ms. Franklin, or Ms. Sheila Calhoun, or any number of other people on board."

My shoulders drooped. "We don't have any, but you must admit the circumstances are suspicious."

"I can't arrest people on things we think happened. I have to have proof. And believe me, the Miami cops will want much more than supposition. Especially with the lawyers and money involved here." He tapped his pencil on his desk.

I squirmed in my seat. I had an idea but wasn't sure I wanted to suggest it. Rob would hate it, but we needed to find a way out of this conundrum. "Um."

Rob and Officer Patterson turned my way.

"I have a plan."

Rob's eyebrow rose.

"Hear me out." I put my hand on Rob's. "I confront her on deck. Tell her I know everything—try to get her to confess." I nodded to the chief security officer, "You could have cameras on me, a microphone, and people standing by to help. I wouldn't be in danger."

"I can do it. I'm not going to let you put yourself in harm's way." Rob squeezed my hand.

I asked the chief security officer. "Who would you be more afraid of? Me," I gestured to my five-foot-four frame and pleasingly plump figure and then hooked a thumb toward Rob, "or him?"

"Doesn't matter. Not risking any passengers' lives on this ship. We've already had one death and one overboard. The captain and line would relieve me of duty if I agreed to this." The chief security officer shook his head.

"So, we're just going to let this killer walk free? That's not right. What if she does it again?"

"Merry, it's not our job to catch her. It's more important you be safe."

"I have a plan where I will be." I outlined it for them.

"There's still an element of risk I'm not happy about." The chief security officer grumbled. "And I'm nuts to agree with this—probably will lose my job..."

He steepled his hands and leaned back on his chair, gazing at the ceiling. "I chose this career because I wanted to make a difference. A childhood friend was killed when we were in our early twenties. I knew his stepfather had done it, but I couldn't prove it, and the police gave up—said they had no case. I swore if I were ever in this situation again, I'd do everything I could to catch the culprit." With a bang, he returned his chair to its normal position and leaned across the desk. "So, if you're willing, I am too."

Rob's teeth ground. "Okay. But if you get injured..."

I smiled even though my stomach was doing backflips. "Then, gentlemen, we are agreed."

Chapter 22

I stood on the top deck, watching the stars glint off the water as we sped northwest toward Florida. I would be happy to leave the ship and see Jenny again. I couldn't wait to hug her.

It was a bit chilly with the wind, so I pulled my white sweater tighter and buttoned the bottom buttons. I would need a large coffee after this—maybe one with whiskey. And cream. Maybe whipped cream.

"Merry, can you hear us?"

I nodded.

"Say something."

"Testing one, two, three..."

"We have sound."

Footsteps approached, and I turned. "Beautiful night, isn't it?"

"Cut the crap. What do you think you know, and why did you drag me out here by myself? Randy snuck from the room to the craps table, and you know how that will end." Sheila wore a red sequined dress with black high heels, making her five foot ten seem even taller.

I couldn't help myself—I shrank against the railing.

A slight breeze arose, and her hair blew into her face—she yanked it behind her ear. "And now my hair will be a wreck. Hurry it up—what's going on?"

I stiffened my shoulders and said, "Found some interesting things about you online. I had no idea you were so talented with computers."

"What do you want? Money? Is this some kind of blackmail?" She took a step closer to me.

"How did you do it? Rob saw the snake, and when the chief security officer lifted the headset, it was gone."

"Butch died of natural causes. That's the official verdict of the doctor. You have nothing." She turned to walk away.

"Michael didn't know Dawn was going to inherit. He found out Butch's will had been changed after he died. His father was the one who had created the new will. Did Michael tell you Randy would inherit?"

"Leave him out of this." She paced. "Michael has nothing to do with—"

"Seems like he has a lot to do with it. How else would you have known what was in the will? I saw you at tea with him, and you seemed a lot closer than just old pals." I was worried she was going to leave—her weight shifted from one foot to the other.

"This is a waste of my time." She spat.

Think, Merry, think. She's a climber—what was it she wanted? "Must have been tough finding out Dawn would get the lion's share of Butch's estate. Were you interested in the company—did you see Randy at the helm?"

"I could care less about the company." She began to walk away.

"Bet you saw yourself as the new mistress of the manor. Probably wanted that house on Long Island. Set yourself up in style. Did you hear Dawn's selling it?"

She stormed toward me, eyes blazing. "That was my house. I loved that house—it was perfect—on the promontory with the ocean surrounding it. My parents lived there once—back before they divorced. Until I was sixteen, I had it made. Michael and all of my school friends lived nearby. I had everything I wanted.

"Then, it all fell apart. Dad made bad decisions, and the creditors came after him—that started the fighting between my parents, and everything went south. Dad was forced to sell, and he sold it cheap. To Randy's mother. And then Butch got it when she died. I waited. I wanted it back—tried to buy it from Butch before we came on this trip.

He just laughed. Said Randy would inherit it eventually—I would just have to wait. Then he leaves it to Dawn." She shook her head. "Unbelievable. Probably did it out of spite."

"I could see how that would make you mad."

She stared past me at the ocean, almost in a trance, like she was talking to herself. "I went from having everything I wanted to my parents divorced and living between them in places of equal squalor. I made up my mind I would restore all they had and more. And I wasn't going to wait another twenty years for Butch to die."

"How'd you do it?" I said softly, willing her to keep talking.

"Not that difficult—at least not for someone like me. Contracted for a new game with graphics and spliced the code into the existing one over the ship's WiFi. On the first day we were on the ship, I told Randy it was the game all the kids were talking about—so he just had to play it that day. Then, he raved about it to Butch. Butch was always competitive with Randy, so I knew he wouldn't be able to resist trying to get further than Randy had.

"Butch and Dawn made an appointment for the very next day. I waited for the call. And then it happened. So easy. When you called, Randy raced out the door. I was ready, and it would have been perfect if not for that stupid steward. He insisted on refreshing the room just as I was going to erase it, so I was late—he kept asking if we needed fresh towels or a different bar set-up. I waited too long after Randy left—that's why Rob saw it." Her eyes focused, and she seemed to come back to the present. "Where is Rob? You two have been joined at the hip this entire journey."

"Watching a basketball game on satellite. He doesn't have to know what I found out—a girl's gotta have pocket money of her own."

"So, this is a shakedown."

I nodded.

"How much?"

"Forty grand."

She appeared to consider it. Then she sprang forward and tried to throw me over the rail. I clung to the steel post they were attached to as she lifted me by the waist. She pounded on my hands to get me to let go as officers streamed from the doors. I couldn't hold on any longer, and she pushed me over.

Black water churned below, and my breath was knocked out when the harness bit. I dangled from the ship as Rob and the chief security officer pulled the tethering rope to bring me closer to the deck. Then, Rob reached for my pants and lifted me back over the rail. I sank against him. "Didn't think that was going to happen."

He put his arms around me. "Scared the heck out of me, even though I knew you were wearing a harness. She moved so quickly—she caught us off guard."

"Time to go." An officer cuffed Sheila and began to lead her away.

Her neck craned as she turned back toward me. "Your word against mine."

I pulled the microphone from my blouse. "Your word against you."

Chapter 23

I rubbed the bruise developing on my ribcage from the harness as I donned my jeans and polo shirt. I was happy it had broken my fall but could have done without the aftermath. My hands hurt too, but the ice the night before had helped.

Rob came around the corner. "Almost ready?"

"Can't wait to get home."

There was a knock at the door, and Rob opened it. Officer Patterson said, "Bad news, folks. The Federal Bureau of Investigation needs to speak with you. The concierge has moved your flight to tomorrow, and your bags have been sent to a hotel. Needless to say, the cruise line will be picking up the cost." He shook our hands. "Good to meet you both. Hopefully, next time you travel with us, it will be far less eventful."

As Rob shut the door, I sighed. "I knew it was too good to be true. We don't have to give up the room for another half hour—want to sit on the deck?"

Our room was on the port side, so we watched the hordes of workers scurrying about. It seemed like a logistical nightmare—kitchen staff inspecting fruits and foods before being loaded to the left and luggage and other things coming off the ship to the right. I touched Rob's hand as a pine box came out and then crossed myself. "Must be Butch." Dawn, Becky, and Sam walked behind the casket and got into a waiting limousine. "I wonder where Randy and Michael are—never mind. I'm sure they're being held for questioning."

A few minutes later, Sheila was led by two people wearing FBI windbreakers, hands cuffed behind her. Then Randy and Michael followed, all put into different vehicles.

After going through customs, we were escorted to a waiting black SUV and driven to FBI headquarters. Surrounded by a tall gate, the two glass-enclosed structures were reminiscent of ships with triangular shapes on the bow. The lobby was light-filled and appeared to soar with blue-green glass panels. We were escorted to a far more unassuming inside conference room to wait.

I turned to Rob, "I miss Jenny. And my cats. I can't believe we have to stay here another night."

"We'll be home soon." He kissed me.

The door opened, and a special agent walked in and introduced herself. We shared everything we knew.

"So, you believe Sheila Calhoun caused her father-in-law, Butch Calhoun, to have a heart attack?"

"And tried to kill me. The cruise ship has the tape. But we also believe she may have tried to kill her husband by cutting his zip line and tried to kill her sister-in-law by throwing her overboard."

"Explain it to me again."

"We believe Sheila was under the mistaken impression her father-in-law, Butch, was going to leave everything to her husband, Randy, including the house she wanted so desperately. She was friendly with the family attorney's son, and he was unaware a new will had been made."

"How did you find that out?"

"Her husband Randy told me."

She jotted a note. "Continue."

"After Butch died, there was a lot of confusion about who got what. When Michael, the attorney on the ship, called his head office, they informed him of the new will and sent him a copy." I doodled on the pad in front of me.

"And how did Ms. Calhoun know this 'Michael?'"

"Family friends, and they dated at one time. They may still be close," Rob said.

"Talk to me about the zip line incident. Why would Ms. Calhoun want to kill her husband?"

"Not sure. A few theories—she was tired of him and wanted to move on, and-or she wanted the money he was supposed to get. After all, he did inherit forty percent, and the company is worth a lot. She could have cut through the harness while standing next to him."

"Or Randy was overweight and fell," Rob interjected.

I shrugged. "That could also be true."

"What about Dawn Franklin's poisoning?"

"That was Randy. He confessed on stage with everyone watching."

The special agent chuckled. "I heard about that from the cruise line's chief security officer. Don't see that happening every day."

I rubbed the back of my neck. "If the house was what she wanted, why would she try and kill Randy? And Becky? What would she gain?"

"The house," the special agent said.

"What?" Rob and I spoke in unison.

"We've been investigating this after hearing Ms. Calhoun's taped confession from the night she tried to kill you and in questioning Michael Grant. A trust Ms. Calhoun owns was negotiating with Ms. Franklin to purchase the house."

"Sheila was the buyer for the house?" My mouth dropped.

"And she needed money to close. We've seen her accounts. She didn't have enough cash. But if she killed her husband, she would get it."

"And Becky?"

"Becky Calhoun hadn't yet gotten around to naming her fiancée, Sam Church, as her beneficiary. That meant Randy would have inherited what Butch had left her. Luckily, they all used the same law firm, and Michael Grant has been very forthcoming about the intricacies of the family wills and trusts."

"But then why wouldn't she have tried to kill Becky first? Why try and kill Randy first—it doesn't seem like it's in the right order."

"Again, we don't have proof she did try to kill her husband. We sent agents to the island but don't have that report yet. This is going to take a while to unravel."

"What about Michael? Was he in on it with Sheila?" I asked.

"Still investigating. As I said, he's been very cooperative. He insists he was unaware she killed Butch Calhoun. He admitted being indiscreet in telling her about Butch Calhoun and Becky Calhoun's wills but said he had no inkling about what she was planning. He maintains he thought Mr. Calhoun's death was from natural causes. We'll see how everything unfolds." The special agent stood. "Thank you for your help—I hope you enjoy the rest of your stay in Miami. We'll be in touch if we need further information and if you think of anything else, please contact me." She handed Rob and me one of her cards, and we followed another agent back to the car.

As the agent drove, I asked Rob, "Do you think Michael was in on it? Or Randy?"

"Not sure about Michael—he certainly has things to answer for. As far as Randy? It's a stretch to think he would want to kill his father and his sister. On the other hand, his wife was expensive to keep happy, and there seemed to be unresolved issues between him and his father."

I gazed out the window. "What a pretty tower—kind of Mediterranean—that place looks old."

The agent who was driving said, "Nearing a century. One of the top hotels in the area."

"It's so old—has history. Wish we were staying there."

"Good thing because that's where we are going." The agent made a turn into the long palm tree-lined drive.

Rob smiled. "This is nice. I thought we'd be at a little hotel near the airport."

"Rather be here," I quipped.

The valet opened the door. "Welcome, Ms. March and Mr. Jenson. I hope you enjoy your stay with us."

We thanked the agent and followed the valet into the lobby. I stopped, stunned at the Moroccan décor. The immense wooden coffered ceilings were stenciled with delicate designs, and the lobby was packed with plush azure and green furniture. It was colorful without being tacky.

"This is breathtaking." I squeezed Rob's hand.

A woman approached. "Good afternoon, Ms. March and Mr. Jenson. I'm the hotel manager—there's no need to check in—that's all arranged. Your private elevator is this way." She led us to a tropical plant-filled atrium.

Rob mouthed, "Private elevator?"

I shrugged.

She stepped in, and we joined her. "I hope your day has been going well. I think you'll love this room. It's our most exclusive."

My eyes widened as the elevator binged, and we stepped out into a large two-story room that would have been right at home in a mansion. A fireplace dominated, with two full-sized gold sofas flanking. Brown leather chairs sat on either side, and the fretwork of the black wrought-iron railing surrounding the open second floor was exquisite.

"Are you sure this isn't another lobby?" Rob murmured.

She showed us into a room with a bed cloaked in white linens that promised to be as comfortable as a cloud. "The bathroom is in there." She pointed to a double door.

I opened it to reveal a shower for two with multiple heads and jets and a sparkling white soaking tub. I smiled, thinking of the bath in my future as we walked back into the living room. The manager pointed to another corner of the room and said, "There's champagne chilling in the bucket and a full bar over there. I know it's getting late for the sun, but you have a cabana reserved by the pool, should you wish to go. Any questions—is there anything else you need?"

"I don't suppose you know what happened to our luggage?" I asked.

"In the closet. Your flight is at eleven tomorrow, and the valet will come and take you to your limo at nine."

She shook our hands and gave us her card. "Call me anytime if you need anything. Thank you for choosing our hotel."

The elevator descended with her in it.

"Only one night? I guess it will have to be enough." Two immense floral displays were on the walnut coffee table situated between the two sofas. One from the cruise line said, "Enjoy the room." The other was from Dawn. "Thanks—I'll be in touch."

Rob said, "Huh. Wonder what that means."

"Care to do the honors?" I peeled the foil from the Perrier Jouet. "My favorite."

Rob popped the cork, poured the champagne, and handed me a glass. "To my brilliant wife."

"To my loving husband." He sat, and I took pictures of the room.

"What are you doing?"

"Want to send these to Jenny." I attached the pictures to a text.

She responded immediately: "That's a room?"

"Yep."

"Can we go there next year?"

I sent a laughing emoji and added: "Can't wait to see you tomorrow."

"I wouldn't come back." Jenny added a heart.

I plopped next to Rob and sipped champagne. "What do you want to do? It's getting late, though I like the idea of our own cabana."

"You want to leave all this?" He swept his arm to encompass the room.

"Nope. But I do want to see how comfortable that bed is."

He stood and held out his hand. "Thought you'd never ask."

Chapter 24

The cruise line had somehow upgraded us to first class for the flight, so Rob enjoyed the extra legroom, and I enjoyed a last glass of champagne. "This was a perfect honeymoon." I kissed his cheek.

"I'm thinking we need another vacation to recover from it." He laughed.

"Not a bad idea. But I'm not sure I'll be ready to leave Jenny again for a while. I hope everything's been okay with Drew and Arianna being there." I frowned.

"Hey—we said no worrying about Drew." He tapped my nose.

"The deal was until the end of our honeymoon."

"By my calculations, it's not over till the plane lands and reality intrudes once more." Rob lifted his book. "And we have about a half hour left. Read your book—no obsessing."

I said a silent prayer that Drew behaved himself while we were gone and would leave town soon after we returned.

When we landed, I hurried toward baggage claim. Jenny held a sign saying, "Welcome Back, Honeymooners."

I ran to her and gave her a big hug. "It's so good to see you. I can't wait to show you all the stuff we bought."

"Me either." She grinned and then hugged Rob. "Great to see you, Rad. Did you have a good time?"

"With your mom? Never a bad time." He shook our neighbor, Andy's, hand. "Thanks for coming with Jenny to pick us up."

"I can't wait to hear about your trip. I want all the details," Andy said. "Well, maybe not all the details, but you know what I mean."

"We have a lot to tell." I hooked my arm through Andy's as we walked toward the door. "And what's been going on here?"

Jenny and Andy exchanged a glance, and he said, "You want to tell her?"

"Uh." Jenny paused, and my heart skipped a beat.

"What happened? It's your dad, isn't it?"

"He left."

"What do you mean he left? How could he leave? When we went on our honeymoon, he had an ankle monitor on. He said he couldn't leave town." I could feel my color start to rise.

Rob rubbed my back. "It's okay."

"I decided to surprise him and Arianna with scones I made myself. When I got to the house, I knocked, but the door was unlocked. When I walked in, the ankle bracelet was on the floor near the kitchen, and he and Arianna were gone. Everything else looked fine, so I wasn't sure what to do. I called Ms. Twilliger, and she came over and called the police." Jenny sniffled. "They said he replaced the SIM card that controls the unit and then cut it off. I haven't heard from them since. I hope he's okay."

"Why is everyone more tech-savvy than me?" I groused. "When did this happen?"

"Five days ago," Andy said.

"Jenny, I talked to you and Patty. Why didn't either one of you tell me about this?" I asked.

Rob and Andy loaded the suitcases into the car, and Jenny shrugged. "You couldn't do anything about it, and we didn't want to ruin your honeymoon."

"I'll always be there for you—you can call me anytime. I'm sorry you had to deal with this alone." I hugged her.

"I wasn't on my own. Ms. Twilliger was with me and let me stay with Cindy, and when Mr. Wall and Mr. Perkins found out what happened, they came over too." Jenny explained.

"Still."

Rob and Andy hopped into the front seats, leaving the back for Jenny and me. I said, "I'm glad we have such good friends. Thanks, Andy."

Rob echoed my sentiment.

* * *

"It's been a month. I can't believe Dad hasn't gotten in touch with me since that one note saying he and Arianna were okay. He said he'd let me know when they got settled. How long does that take?" Jenny complained.

"I've never fled the law, so I can't answer that question. Did you get the mail?" I asked.

She walked to the counter and picked up a handful of items. "Got this from some legal firm. Big envelope."

"Hope this isn't something else your father's gotten into." I said a quick novena as I opened the package. "Huh. It isn't that at all."

Jenny sank onto a chair next to me. "What is it?"

"Something that means we don't have to worry about your tuition. Remember my telling you about the woman whose husband died on the cruise?"

She nodded.

"Well, she set up an educational trust for you to thank us for uncovering what happened. I wonder if we should accept."

"Are you nuts? The board supported her and let her get rid of Randy when they found out what happened, so she ended up with sole control of the company. Not to mention the fact that her stepdaughter-in-law tried to kill you. She has the money, and you earned it. I say we keep it."

Jenny licked her lips. "We should celebrate at Fiorella's. Can Jacob come?"

I laughed. "Why not?"

ABOUT THE AUTHOR

Eileen Curley Hammond is an author who retired from a successful marketing career in the insurance industry. She and her husband share the house with two cats that are having a hard time training them.

For those of you who have been keeping up on this page, you know that Eileen and her husband restocked the fish pond last year with koi, shubunkins, and minnows. They are still happily swimming in peace with screens and motion sensors guarding their kingdom.

It's been such a blessing to be able to travel and be with people again. I wish you and the ones you love all the best.